"I'm afraid of you," Rachel said.

She felt Shade's hands moving up and down her back and tried not to think how they felt as if they belonged there. "Of myself." She lifted her own hands to his shoulders. "Of us."

"Join the club." His hands drifted below her waist, settling on her hips, drawing her closer.

She tilted her head back and looked up at him. "Are you saying—"

"I'm afraid of us, too.

"I dream of you, dammit!" He grabbed hold of her slender hand that had been stroking his face, then found, to his distraction, that he couldn't let go. "I think of you when I should be planning how I'm going to get into that damn prison. I can't afford any distractions right now. Yet I can't stop wondering what it is about you that's gotten under my skin. What secret you possess that makes you so different from *any* woman I've ever known...."

JoAnn Ross is one of Temptation's most popular and prolific authors—and the sheer scope of the kinds of stories she writes explains why. From intrigues to swashbuckling alien adventures to sensual dramas, JoAnn does it all. *Angel of Desire* is a delightful tale of two very star-crossed lovers. In June, JoAnn weaves an emotionally compelling story with *The Return of Caine O'Halloran,* the first book in our Lost Loves miniseries. (What if you had the chance to fall in love all over again? Would you?)

Books by JoAnn Ross

HARLEQUIN TEMPTATION

382–DARK DESIRES
409–THE KNIGHT IN SHINING ARMOR
432–STAR-CROSSED LOVERS
436–MOONSTRUCK LOVERS
453–THE PRINCE AND THE SHOWGIRL
471–LOVESTORM

ANGEL OF DESIRE

JoANN ROSS

Harlequin Books

TORONTO • NEW YORK • LONDON
AMSTERDAM • PARIS • SYDNEY • HAMBURG
STOCKHOLM • ATHENS • TOKYO • MILAN
MADRID • WARSAW • BUDAPEST • AUCKLAND

To Shelley Mosley and Julie Havir
For their friendship and years of
lunches yet to come

ISBN 0-373-25582-9

ANGEL OF DESIRE

This edition published by arrangement with Harlequin Enterprises B. V.

Printed in U.S.A.

Prologue

IT WAS CHRISTMAS DAY. The Vermont sky was dark and gloomy, the air so cold the icy crystals literally stole one's breath away. Prudent people were indoors with their families, feasting on roast turkey and cranberry sauce and pumpkin pie.

But the youthful residents of the Vermont boys' home had no families. And dinner, while an admitted improvement over everyday fare, had been less than festive. The younger boys had cried; the older boys, who might have secretly wanted to weep, as well, exhibited stoic faces.

They'd sat through the lengthy morning church service, raced through the obligatory grace, wolfed down the baked ham and candied sweet potatoes and had finally been freed to work out their anger and unhappiness on the frozen lake behind the rambling three-story brick orphanage.

While a rigorous hockey game was taking place on the ice, two eleven-year-old boys, one clad in a hand-me-down smoke-gray parka that matched the lowering sky, the other in a blue as bright as a jay's wing, straddled a log beneath a towering pine tree. It was snowing—white flakes that swirled in the frosty air, so thick it was nearly impossible to see the other bank of the lake.

The boy in gray took a red Swiss army knife from the pocket of his parka and without so much as wincing once, sliced a neat line across the tip of his left index finger. He solemnly handed the knife to the other boy, who did the same. Unwilling tears of self-inflicted pain glistened momentarily in the second boy's bright blue eyes.

They touched fingertips.

"Now we're brothers," the first boy declared. "Forever."

"Forever," the second boy agreed, immensely grateful to have found this friend who had made his sudden parentless state a great deal less bleak.

At eleven, they realized that the odds of them ever being adopted were slim to none. That being the case, the two boys—one who'd been abandoned by his alcoholic mother years ago, the other who'd recently lost his parents in a fiery car crash—had decided to adopt each other.

The blood staining the two fingertips congealed quickly in the cold afternoon air. The brief ceremony concluded, the boys skated back out onto the ice and rejoined the hockey game in progress.

The puck was a black bullet moving over the frozen lake like a penny skidding across a newly waxed floor. The boy in gray trapped it momentarily with his stick, then took off across the lake, skating in long, self-assured strides. The December wind howled and the snow fell in a thick white curtain, obscuring his vision. Intent on making this goal, he failed to hear the ice cracking beneath the serrated steel runners of his skates.

Nor did he see the jagged fissure widening in front of him.

The fragile ice gave way, sounding like shattering crystal. One minute the boy was streaking across the surface of the lake, a long-legged gray blur; the next minute he found himself sinking lower and lower, surrounded by cold dark water.

Refusing to give in to panic, he searched for an escape route, but either the ice had closed behind him, or his momentum had carried him far beyond the opening. The ice over his head was as hard as the granite mountains that hovered over the boys' home.

As icy water began to replace the air in his young lungs, the boy realized he was going to die.

And then, unbelievably, he saw her, swimming toward him, surrounded by a warm golden light, her long hair streaming wetly behind her. Her remarkable eyes, as gray as the ice overhead but a great deal warmer, offered the same calm reassuring comfort as her smile.

As he took her strangely warm, outstretched hand, it crossed his mind that the idea of a mermaid living in a Vermont lake was impossible.

Then the world turned black.

When he woke, he was lying on a cot in the home's infirmary. The doctor, irritated at having been called away from his own children on this holiday, brusquely assured the boy that he'd live, then scolded him for behaving so recklessly.

The boy didn't listen to the lecture; he'd heard it innumerable times over the nearly five years he'd lived in the home.

He glanced around, half-expecting to see his mermaid, unsurprised when he didn't.

His rational mind assured him that she'd only been a hallucination, born from a lack of oxygen to his brain. But then something brushed against his cheek, something as invisible as air, as soft as a pussy willow, as warm as July sunshine.

And as impossible as it might seem, for the first time in his young life, the boy had a fleeting feeling that he was not alone.

1

HIS NAME WAS SHADE. Which suited a man who lived in shadows.

Few people knew him by this name. Indeed, he'd had so many identities over the years that there were times when he wondered if even he, with his eidetic memory, could recall them all. Not that he would want to try.

The man called Shade lived solely for the moment, an inevitable attitude for an individual whose life could end at any time. The work he did was as dangerous as it was secretive, and when a job was completed—successfully, for Shade would have it no other way—he left both the unpleasantness his work entailed, and whatever identity he'd taken on, where it belonged.

In the dark and murky past.

And then, as always, he moved on.

Shade was intelligent, fearless and intrinsically deadly. His exploits, some exaggerated, most not, were the stuff of legends, the kind of tales any spy novelist would kill for.

Before being forced into an early and unwilling retirement, he'd spent six months with the rebels in Afghanistan, had witnessed the breakup of the Baltic Republics, had been on the scene of more than one Caribbean coup, and, more familiar with the Middle East than men twice his age, had successfully infiltrated Baghdad two weeks before the UN forces began dropping their deadly smart bombs on the city.

Some of those who'd worked with him, and lived to tell about it, called him crazy. Others proclaimed him dangerous. Still others had sworn he possessed a death wish and refused to ever team up with him again.

Shade had steadfastly ignored them all. With the exception of one man, who'd become his brother on a long-ago winter day, Shade had never cared what anyone thought. He was a man alone, a cold, distant remote island unto himself. Which was just the way he liked it.

Which was why, when the bureaucratic drones in the government had attempted to bring him in from the cold and plunk him behind the safety of a shiny new desk, he'd promptly quit. He'd given up his guaranteed salary, his generous health plan, his pension, and walked away.

Shade did not look back.

Afterward, his only regret was that he hadn't begun working for himself years earlier.

Shade did not advertise his services. There was no need. His clients, for lack of a better word, consisted of desperate, normally law-abiding individuals who had first attempted to solve their problems by legal means.

But inevitably, after they found themselves hopelessly tangled in a maze of red tape, they would go looking for alternate solutions.

And that's when they found their way to him.

Shade was, quite simply, a gun for hire. A mercenary. An unpretty term for an admittedly unpretty job. He continued to do what he'd always done, but these days he had no one to answer to but himself. No conscience to concern him but his own. Fortunately, his own conscience was not all that troublesome.

He'd kidnapped children who had been spirited out of the United States by foreign spouses from remote hilltop homes that were nearly fortresses and returned them to grateful American parents.

He'd rescued terrified college students thrown into prisons that made medieval dungeons seem homey for the stupid crime of smuggling a Playboy magazine or a bit of homegrown pot into religiously fundamentalist countries.

On three occasions, he arranged escape for women who'd married dashing, dark-eyed sheikhs only to find themselves, once the ceremony was over, deprived of their passports and their rights.

Once, he'd hijacked a plane carrying an elusive Latin-American drug lord to his seaside retreat. After landing the Learjet on a deserted, little-known runway in the desert ten miles east of San Diego, Shade had walked away, leaving his hostage bound and gagged, tied up with a bright red ribbon for the widow of a DEA agent whose husband had been tortured and killed on the drug kingpin's orders.

Knowing that the unlucky agent had left behind six kids, three approaching college age, Shade had refused payment for that particular job. The knowledge that the drug lord was serving a life sentence without parole in a Florida federal penitentiary was satisfaction enough.

Currently between jobs, he was sitting on his deck, booted feet crossed at the ankle on the redwood railing, drinking in the warmth of a benevolent April sun. The air was clear and fresh as only New England air can be in springtime, making him realize that he never took time to even notice the weather unless it threatened to screw up a mission.

The portable radio beside him was tuned to a baseball game. As he drank a beer, he gazed out over the heavily wooded two acres. During the year the house had sat vacant, Mother Nature had stepped in to reclaim the land.

"Place could use some weeding," he decided, eyeing the daffodils struggling valiantly to rise above the dark thorny thicket of weeds.

As he tipped the long-necked bottle back and took a swallow, Shade decided that if Sleeping Beauty had been on the other side of that impenetrable tangle, the prince would have needed one helluva souped-up chain saw to cut his way through to her.

"Then again," he considered, "there's something to be said for the natural look."

This was the first home he'd ever owned. Although he'd had more than his share of misgivings about joining the ranks of the American home owner, the sprawling glass-and-wood home, settled on the banks of a fast-running ribbon of crystal-clear creek, had drawn him like a siren's call. Telling himself that he was only buying the place because of the attractive tax break, he'd signed the final mortgage papers two weeks ago.

At first it had not been easy. Accustomed to apartments and hotel rooms—and a great deal less hospitable conditions when he was working—Shade had found trying to sleep amid so much space an impossibility.

He'd spent the first few nights prowling from empty room to empty room, like a cautious jungle cat staking out new territory in the moonlight slanting through the house's many skylights.

Now, fifteen days later, as he watched a red-breasted robin yank a plump worm from the moist earth of the rockery beside the creek, he realized he was beginning to get used to the idea that this place was his.

It crossed Shade's mind that since the purchase of this house, he no longer awoke each day edgy and primed for danger, a necessary attitude when your line of work routinely got you threatened, beat up and shot at. A job where people lied to you and cheated and tried, with depressing regularity, to kill you; a job where you lied and cheated and sometimes killed.

In fact, truth be told, he was finding the idea of leaving his comfortable new innerspring mattress to sleep on the wet ground in some godforsaken jungle definitely unappealing.

Perhaps he was finally losing it. Now that, Shade decided with a grimace, was a depressing thought. Nearly as depressing as the one that had been stirring in some dark corner of his mind lately—the idea that he might be in danger of turning into a living cliché.

His frown darkening, he popped open another beer, continued to survey the backyard, thought about driving into town and buying some hedge clippers and came to the conclusion that the place had a certain wild charm.

"No point in getting carried away," he decided.

The breeze sighing through the tops of the trees, the babbling of the brook added a soothing counterpoint to the crack of the bat and the roar of the crowd from the radio. Beside the deck, a lilac bush was bravely pushing the season, its early lavender flowers perfuming the April air.

When the doorbell rang, Shade reluctantly pushed himself to his feet, went into the house and made his way across the oak floor to the front door.

"Special delivery. For Shade Blackstone," the uniformed woman said.

"That's me." Figuring it must be one more document to add to the mountain of legalized paperwork buying a home entailed, he signed the sheet, receiving a slim white legal-sized envelope in return.

He grabbed a bag of potato chips from the kitchen counter on the way back to the deck. Then, settling back into the Adirondack chair, he sliced the envelope open with his fingernail.

The advisory, on a single sheet of paper, had been typewritten—on a Selectric, Shade observed on some absent, professional level. You didn't see many typewriters these days. Not with computers on every desk. The paper was the plain white kind that could be purchased in any office supply store. The note, brief and to the point, was unsigned.

The hairs on the back of Shade's neck prickled.

As he scanned the single paragraph, the potato chips, the beer, his tangle of roots and weeds and overgrown grass were all instantly forgotten.

His curse, as he ripped the paper into pieces, was short and savage. His jaw clenched. His eyes blazed with a hot inner fury.

It was noon. By twelve-fifteen, Shade had stuffed some clothes into a well-worn duffel bag and by one o'clock had placed several telephone calls to sources around the world. Three hours after the letter's arrival, he was sitting in the first-class section of a Boeing 737 winging its way south to Washington, D.C.

The flight attendant, a perky redhead with corkscrew curls and long, wraparound legs, brought his drink to him with a bright, professional smile. One look at his granite face and his cold, implacable eyes and her smile faded. Her fingers trembled as she handed him the miniature bottle of Scotch.

Later, she slipped into the cabin to warn the crew of a possible hijacking attempt.

Never, she swore on a shaky voice worlds different from the smooth contralto tones that had given seatbelt instructions prior to takeoff, never had she viewed such murder in a man's eyes.

MURDER. The word tolled warningly, dangerously, in Rachel's mind.

"I cannot let him do it," she insisted for the umpteenth time.

Her superior shrugged and folded his slender, patrician hands atop the glossy ebony surface of his desk. "The man Shade has killed before," he reminded her needlessly.

"Only in self-defense. When his life, and those of others, were in jeopardy."

Joshua gave her a long, stern look over the rim of his silver-framed glasses. He did not need the spectacles, Rachel knew. He wore them for effect. A former actor, Joshua knew how to utilize props to his advantage.

"And this time is different?"

"Very different," she admitted reluctantly. It was not easy to admit that someone she'd cared for so intimately, for so long, could be on the verge of such a deadly act. "I have every reason to believe that he intends to commit cold-blooded murder."

Joshua didn't immediately answer. Instead, he took off the glasses and began folding the stems back and forth in a cautious, thoughtful gesture that had her already keyed-up nerves jangling. The silence lingered, on and on. Patience had never been Rachel's long suit. Today's situation was stretching her self-control to the limit.

"If you are correct," he said finally, putting the glasses back on and giving her a sagacious stare through the clear lenses, "you know what that means."

"Of course I do," Rachel flared. Realizing she'd just broken the rules—again!—she closed her eyes, pressed her generous lips together and prayed for composure.

"Why don't you explain the circumstances to me again," Joshua suggested. This time his voice softened with honest affection.

She'd been assigned to Joshua Brand her first day. Disoriented and distressed, she'd found his calm, steady demeanor instantly comforting. He was a kind and gentle man. An intelligent man. A good friend and an even better teacher.

The one thing he hadn't been able to teach her was patience.

As the years passed, others—those for whom tranquillity came easier—moved on, rising higher and higher in the hierarchy. Rachel's temperament continued to cost her any promotion.

Not that she really minded. She honestly couldn't imagine being any happier than she was, doing work she loved.

Today, however, she was far from happy. Frustration surged through her. Didn't he understand that time was of the essence? Although it took every ounce of self-restraint Rachel possessed, she managed to keep from suggesting that they save the lengthy, drawn-out explanations for later.

She took a deep breath. "Shade never knew his father," she began, schooling her voice to a calm she was a very long way from feeling. "His mother drank. Heavily. He became a ward of Vermont State when he was seven years old."

"An unfortunate beginning," Joshua allowed.

"Very." She remembered how she'd cried for the abandoned young boy. "When he was eleven, he became friends with another boy who'd been orphaned."

"Conlan O'Donahue," Joshua's long, perfectly manicured fingers tapped across the computer keys. "His parents were killed in a car crash. Since there were no relatives to take him in, he was placed in the Vermont boys' home."

Rachel wondered why she need go over this when Joshua had the information right there in his all-knowing computer.

"That's right. Although Shade was a loner, even as a child, the two boys hit it off. They even became blood brothers."

"That was the day Shade almost drowned," Joshua recalled.

Soft color drifted into Rachel's cheeks. Trust her superior to remember that. She wondered if Joshua also remembered their heated argument afterward and knew that he did.

"That's right," she murmured reluctantly.

Rather than remind her of her greatest indiscretion, Joshua returned his attention to the computer. "Conlan O'Donahue appears to have been a mirror image of his friend. Where Shade ran away from school with distressing regularity, Conlan enjoyed his classes and earned straight *A*s."

"Shade was every bit as intelligent," Rachel interjected loyally. "He merely had trouble with rules and regulations."

"A problem that seems to continue, even now," the older man mused. Rachel didn't respond. "They both went to college."

"Shade went to Notre Dame on a football scholarship, Conlan went to Harvard as a merit scholar."

"Yes." Joshua nodded his silver head. "That's exactly what it says. After graduation, your man went to work for the government. In intelligence." His slight frown suggested his distaste for any career that required a talent for prevarication.

"The major part of Shade's salary went to help pay Conlan's way through medical school," Rachel said.

Shade's hefty contribution to his friend's lean financial coffers had been an extremely generous act. And right now, Shade needed all the points he could earn. His life's slate, seemingly filled with more bad than good, did not reveal the true man Rachel knew him to be.

"A generous gesture," Joshua allowed.

"Very generous." Her emphatic tone earned another quick, probing look from the man who'd begun as her teacher and had become her dearest friend.

It was, of course, against the rules to become emotionally involved with Shade. He was, Joshua had reminded her on more than one occasion, merely an assignment. A very important assignment, granted, but when the time came to move on, as it always did, she would be required to direct all her attention to her new subject.

"Without the enormous debt most doctors have when they finish school, Conlan was able to follow his dream to use medicine to help others."

"His work for the International Rescue the Children Fund has been quite impressive," Joshua murmured as the list of Conlan O'Donahue's achievements flashed across the screen. Page after page of them.

Seeing them in black and white like this, Rachel understood why, on those rare occasions when Shade compared himself with his blood brother, he felt he came up depressingly short.

She had never believed that, of course. But Rachel understood all too well that emotions and truth were not always the same thing. Her own life had been proof of that.

"Conlan is a wonderful doctor. And a wonderful person," she agreed. It was true. "Not to mention being a loving and devoted husband." He'd married a pediatrician he'd met during residency, Rachel remembered.

"Who's about to become a father."

"Really?" She leaned forward in an attempt to read the screen. "I didn't know that."

"Neither does he. For that matter, neither does his wife." More tapping on the keys. The screen changed. "She will find out today."

Rachel let out a long breath. "The same day she learns her husband's been taken captive by government troops in Yaznovia." Talk about your good news, bad news, she considered. "According to the anonymous letter Shade just received, Conlan has been arrested and accused of working with the rebels."

She didn't add that those same rebels were being called freedom fighters by every legitimate government in the free world. Joshua had never been at all political. And, of course, it was against policy to enter into disputes between the world's battling nations.

"That's only the military government's excuse," he said, surprising her with his knowledge of the actual situation. "In truth, they have a far more sinister agenda."

Four years ago, General Rutskoya, president-for-life of the eastern European Alpine country, had orchestrated a series of massacres in remote, mountainous refugee camps.

The battalion in charge of the massacre, led by the general's brother, was eventually infiltrated by Shade. And although his actions had not resulted in the downfall of the brutal military regime, it had brought the atrocities into the world spotlight, resulting in immediate economic sanctions.

After months of oppressive rule, Yaznovia was finally viewed in its true colors: an outlaw nation, run by outlaws.

That had been Shade's last official assignment for the U.S. government. He'd been gravely wounded in an ambush and had lingered in that smoky netherworld between life and death for weeks. Afterward, when his cover had been blown by a traitor, he'd been tortured by the general's henchmen while the ruler himself watched.

Eventually Shade had escaped his tormentors. But not before being forced to kill the general's brother.

"A brother for a brother," Rachel whispered as the evil enormity of the situation sank in.

"Exactly." Joshua's rewarding smile was grim. "Except in this case, General Rutskoya plans to lure your Shade into his snare, using Conlan as bait. Then he intends to kill them both."

Dear Lord, this was even worse than she'd thought. "Please, Joshua, you must let me go to Shade. To help him." Bright color waved like scarlet flags in her delicate, too-pale cheeks.

"You know I cannot allow that. Your place is here, Rachel." Harsh lines carved their way across her superior's aristocratic brow.

"My place is helping Shade." Her gray eyes, fringed by a row of long smoky lashes, pleaded. Her normally throaty voice was husky with pent-up emotion. "You chose him for me, Joshua, from the moment he took his first breath."

Rachel, formerly Rachel Parrish of Salem, Massachusetts, an outspoken, untraditional midwife who'd been unjustly hanged in 1692 as a witch, had been Shade's guardian angel for all of his sometimes stormy, always rocky thirty-five years.

She'd pulled him from the freezing water that long-ago winter day when he'd fallen through the ice, and although it certainly hadn't been easy, given Shade's unfortunate and reckless lack of concern for his own life, she'd rescued him from innumerable dangerous situations.

And although she hadn't been able to keep him from being severely wounded during that ambush in the mountains, and she'd been forced to watch as he'd been brutally tortured, she had managed—just barely—to keep him alive.

"You've saved the man's life many times without taking on earthly bonds," Joshua reminded her needlessly.

She was grateful when he didn't bring up that one time—when Shade was eleven—when she'd panicked and taken matters into her own hands by returning to the mortal world without first seeking the required permission.

"You have to understand." Unable to sit still another moment, she sprang to her feet and leaned over the desk, desperately pressing her point. "It's not Shade's life I'm worried about saving, Joshua."

Rachel shivered as she thought of the intent she'd witnessed in Shade's eyes to commit premeditated, cold-blooded murder.

"It's his soul."

2

AS SOON AS HE ARRIVED in the city, Shade went straight to the Capitol Hill town house of his best—and only—friend. He was relieved when Marianne O'Donahue, Conlan's wife, displaying the grit that Shade had always admired and Con had loved, did not succumb to hysterics upon learning of her husband's capture.

"After all," Marianne reminded him in the smooth round tones that betrayed her Boston roots, "Con and I both knew and accepted the risks involved."

The Rescue the Children Fund was an international, nonprofit agency, famous for operating in places that the average SWAT team wouldn't dare go. Working together as a team, Marianne and Conlan had dispensed medical assistance, as well as comfort and love, in many of the same hot spots where Shade had worked undercover. The national offices of the Rescue the Children Fund were in Washington, as was Marianne and Con's home, but they only returned to the States for a few weeks every year.

"The thing I find frustrating," Marianne told Shade, "is that I can't be with Con when he needs me the most." She shook her head. "I returned to Washington to shore up some needed funding and support for our relief work in Yaznovia. Perhaps, if I'd stayed with him . . ."

"If you were with Con, I'd have to figure out some way to get two people out of prison instead of one," Shade answered.

She smiled at that, a sweet, brave smile that only wobbled slightly. "Dear Shade." She covered his dark hand with her own. "Con couldn't have asked for a better brother." Mutinous tears filled her eyes. "I'm sorry." A single tear fell; she brushed it impatiently away. "Dammit, I'm not usually so weepy."

"Hey, you're entitled."

Marianne sighed. "Perhaps it's better I did come back here to the States last week," she mused out loud. "Because even though he's a brilliant doctor, I have a feeling that Con would waste precious time and mental energy worrying about my condition. And Lord knows, he certainly has enough to be concerned about right now."

"Your condition?" Comprehension hit with the force of a neutron bomb. Shade's startled glance slid to her flat stomach.

"I'm going to have a baby," Marianne announced with obvious feminine pride. "Con and I are going to be parents by Christmas. Which makes you, Shade—" she reached over and kissed his cheek "—an uncle-to-be."

That little bombshell sent Shade reeling. The idea of Conlan becoming a father stirred something deep inside him. Something he would not—could not—recognize as envy. Assuring his best friend's wife that he'd get her husband out of Yaznovia safely, Shade took her up on her invitation to stay for dinner, although she had to laughingly chase him out of the kitchen, accusing him of hovering around her as if he expected her to go into labor at any moment.

Over chicken curry, saffron rice and beer, he told her about his house, of the nightmarish closing, of the jungle yard that could serve as a location shoot for any Tarzan movie, of the family of raccoons that had set up housekeeping in the kitchen.

"You're lying about the raccoons," she accused, wiping away tears—this time born of laughter—with the backs of her hands.

"The hell I am." His lips curved into an uncharacteristic, seldom-used smile. "I evicted the little rascals the first day, but they refused to leave the property. When I left for the airport, they were sulking somewhere beneath the deck."

He'd purposefully exaggerated, rewarded each time her freckled face blossomed into that dazzling smile that had made Conlan fall in love with the lively pediatrician.

After allowing himself to be talked out of going to a hotel, he spent the night in the small but comfortable guest room.

The following day he visited old haunts, gathering all the information he could on the situation in Yaznovia. Neither Shade nor his informants worried overly much about the classified briefings given to him, a civilian, as being technically illegal. In the shadowy world of international espionage, the lines of legality and morality often blurred.

After his meetings, Shade had the gist of the problem, and the beginning of an admittedly sketchy plan. And as much as he wanted to leave for Yaznovia immediately, he was forced to cool his heels while a cadre of professionals created the passport and various papers that would give him a new identity. An identity that would not only get him into the renegade country but would actually make him a welcome visitor.

He was frustrated, impatient and in a generally lousy mood when he dropped into a bar in Washington, D.C.'s Union Station. The Beaux Arts building had been designed as a monumental public entrance to the nation's capital back in the days when passenger trains had been a luxurious way to travel.

After falling into decades of disrepair, the building had been successfully remodeled to include upscale shops, restaurants and drinking holes for all the bureaucrats working on Capitol Hill. This particular bar was in transition, having originated as an eighties' fern bar, only to become a *faux* Irish pub, and from what he could tell, was on its way to retro urban cowboy.

The western look extended to the customers—eager, upwardly mobile congressional staffers and intense, single-minded lobbyists. Several of the men had taken to wearing boots and bolo ties with their navy business suits. Revealing a bias toward this youthful clientele, the jukebox offered up stars like Randy Travis, Clint Black and Billy Ray Cyrus, with only an occasional nod to old-timers like Waylon and Willie and Merle.

"Times," Shade muttered to himself when a lissome young thing dressed in fringe and leather played "Achy Breaky Heart" for the third time, "are definitely achanging." And not, he considered, wishing for just one chorus of "Bar Room Buddies," necessarily for the better.

"You're tellin' me, buddy," the bartender, a man two decades older than his customers, muttered as he mixed up a blender of fluffy pastel drinks. "These kids wouldn't know real country music if Johnny Cash himself suddenly strolled in that door and began belting out 'Orange Blossom Special.'"

The bartender poured strawberry daiquiris into a pair of frosted glasses. "And they damn sure wouldn't recognize a real drink if it bit them on their designer denim asses." After nodding his head approvingly in the direction of Shade's Scotch, he headed off to the other end of the bar to take an order from a cocktail waitress dressed like Dale Evans.

Damn, Shade thought, as he nursed his drink and slapped at the leafy Boston fern that kept brushing his head, the thing he hated most about this work was the waiting.

COMPARED TO THE bright spring sunshine outside, the bar was as dark as a cave. Rachel stood in the doorway and blinked twice, willing her eyes to adjust to the dim lighting.

Finally she saw Shade at the far end of the bar, brooding beneath a huge fern. His broad shoulders were hunched as he bent over his drink, and he was staring into the Scotch as if seeking the answers to the universe in its amber depths. He was alone, isolated in his dark thoughts. Finding the burden of her mortal body unexpectedly cumbersome after all these years, Rachel edged her way toward him, through the crowd of attractive, enthusiastic young people.

She came to a stop behind his left shoulder and waited.

Nothing.

He took a swallow, ignoring her so completely she might have been invisible. As she admittedly had been on so many occasions when she'd felt it necessary to enter his life.

She murmured a soft, polite ahem.

Still nothing.

"Excuse me," she murmured, placing a hand on his shoulder.

That was a mistake. Shade was off the bar stool like a rocket shot, one wide hand raised to strike, the other reaching beneath his leather jacket. The expression on his chiseled face was definitely not welcoming. Well, at least she'd gotten his attention.

"I'm so sorry," she gasped as she was forced to look a long, long way up. She'd known he was tall, known that he topped most men by several inches, but she'd never before experienced the sheer power exuding from his body. It affected her like a physical assault.

The solitary little boy she'd once rescued from an icy grave had grown into a very large man. But she'd recognize that cautious, almost belligerent scowl anywhere. A thin white line encircled his lips and his face was as dark and potentially dangerous as a thundercloud. Beneath his sable hair, his eyes were as green as newly mined emeralds. And every bit as hard. A faint white line slashed its jagged way up his dark cheek, giving him a rakish, dangerous look.

"I didn't mean to surprise you."

Her gray eyes were wide and startled, but Shade saw no fear in them.

Her complexion was the almost mythical ivory classical writers had rhapsodized over. The kind of face, he considered fleetingly, that could have been plucked from a Renaissance painting of an angel on the gilded ceilings of all those Florentine cathedrals.

Her unadorned eyes—wide, innocent eyes laced with quiet strength—were thickly lashed, and her full, pouty lips, which had parted on a surprised gasp, appeared as soft and pink as a cherub's.

Taking in her attire—a decidedly unchic, starkly tailored black suit and practical, low-heeled shoes—he decided that she must be a companion to the two nuns who'd been standing outside the station, soliciting donations for the homeless.

He dug into a pocket, pulled out a stack of bills, peeled off a twenty. "Here you go, Sister. Put it to good use." The first pair had promised to pray for him, which had been a nice enough idea, but Shade wasn't holding out any hope for redemption.

Rachel, too, had noticed the nuns. She'd also observed Shade put fifty dollars into the donation basket. "I'm afraid you're mistaken." She smiled at his error, thinking she'd come a very long way in three hundred years. From a witch to a nun.

His gaze sharpened. "You're not a nun?"

"No. Were you, perhaps, seeking a nun?"

"In this place?" His lips quirked at one corner. "Hardly."

A little silence settled over them as each studied the other.

"So, who are you?" Shade asked. "And what do you want?"

Unfortunately, there was no easy answer to his second question. Although Joshua had warned her against revealing her identity, lying was also prohibited.

"Perhaps we could discuss it over a drink?" Rachel had never drunk alcohol. But surely the bartender would know how to brew a cup of tea.

Hell. So she was just another woman looking to get picked up. Telling himself that he'd overreacted, Shade relaxed. Slightly.

He ran his eyes over her with deliberate slowness. From the top of her gleaming head down to her feet, clad in sensible shoes. When that unnervingly thorough gaze lingered on her breasts, her throat grew arid and she had a sudden urge to cover them with her hands. An urge she resisted. Instead, she kept her arms stiffly at her sides, defiantly tilted her chin and submitted herself to his cool male study.

She definitely wasn't his type. Oh, the woman was attractive enough in a straightforward, unadorned sort of way, with her shiny, neat honey hair and wide, intelligent gray eyes. And although her black suit was too starkly tailored for his taste, beneath the lightweight wool jacket he could detect some very appealing, very feminine curves.

Under normal circumstances, he might find it intriguing to peel off that conservative nun's habit to discover what she was wearing underneath. Experience had taught him that the more sedate an image a woman projected to the world, the more likely she was to favor frothy confections of lace and silk beneath that carefully created facade.

But these were far from normal circumstances. And he couldn't allow himself to get distracted by a friendly blonde. Even one who seemed vaguely familiar.

"Sorry, Sister, but I'm afraid I wouldn't be very good company tonight." He flashed her a savage grin that possessed neither warmth nor humor.

Bright color flooded into Rachel's cheeks as she realized he'd mistaken her for the type of woman who would tumble willingly, enthusiastically, into his bed. That forbidden idea created a flare of bright starlight heat; she felt as if all her nerve endings were being pricked by the star's sharp points.

Embarrassed, she attempted to gather her scattered thoughts, reminding herself of her mission.

"Oh, but I wasn't looking for company." Rachel had never been anything if not tenacious. Indeed, her very strong streak of stubbornness, unseemly maidenly behavior in 1692 Salem, had been more than a little responsible for her fate. "Actually, I had conversation in mind."

"If you want conversation, try the bartender," he suggested. "He gets paid to talk to customers."

Having been by his side for all of his thirty-five years, Rachel, of all people, should have known exactly how brusque and unfriendly Shade could be. Especially when his mind was on a mission. She'd seen his tongue practically strip the hide off a superior attempting to rein him in, and over the years she'd watched him reduce more than one intelligent, successful woman to tears when the job was done and it came time to move on.

Understanding that he was not nearly as bereft of feelings as he liked to believe, she'd always overlooked his cynical attitude and uncaring behavior. But never had she expected the pain of rejection to sting quite so badly.

Chiding herself for allowing a prick of very feminine and very mortal pique to get beneath her skin, she squared her shoulders and tried again.

"I don't want to talk to the bartender. I wish to speak with you."

He'd returned to his Scotch, but her no-nonsense tone garnered his reluctant attention. He spun around on the stool and gave her another, longer look. As Kathy Mattea started "Burnin' Old Memories" on the jukebox, he felt another distant tug of remembrance. He cursed softly. "Look, if it's about hiring me, I'm kind of tied up right now with other things."

"I know. And those other things are exactly what I wish to discuss with you."

His gaze sharpened. "You're not from Tony?"

Tony Bendetti had been arrested ten years ago for securities fraud and forgery. Not that there had been anything wrong with his work; if anything, under close scrutiny, his phony stock certificates had looked better than the originals.

Unfortunately, when he'd broken up with his girlfriend shortly after floating the bad paper, she'd taken a handful of the certificates to the Feds, who, recognizing talent when they saw it, had offered Tony a deal he couldn't refuse. They'd keep him out of prison if he came to work for them.

The partnership had proven mutually rewarding. Tony avoided spending ten to fifteen years behind bars and the intelligence community had their very own Michelangelo. The last three passports Tony had created for Shade had been masterpieces.

This woman certainly didn't look like one of Tony's usual delivery girls.

"No." She shook her head, dislodging a long spiral curl from the tidy knot at the nape of her neck. The silken strand brushed against her neck, appearing like honey on cream. "I'm not from Tony Bendetti."

Shade knew damn well he hadn't told her Tony's last name. "But you know him."

His right hand lifted the glass to his lips while his left moved instinctively to his belt to reassure himself that his 9 mm semiautomatic pistol was safely nestled against the small of his back.

She still looked harmless. But in his business a guy who took anyone at face value, especially an attractive woman who smelled like heaven, inevitably ended up laid out on a slab with a tag on his big toe.

As they faced each other, the music, the lull of happy-hour conversations, the laughter faded into the distance. At this moment, they could have been the only two people in the bar. The air around them was practically crackling.

"I don't know him personally. But I do know who Tony Bendetti is. I am also acquainted with his line of work."

Tension shimmered between them. Shade was all barely restrained energy, reminding Rachel of a jungle cat prepared to pounce. His green eyes glittered dangerously.

"May I make a suggestion?" she asked quietly.

"What?"

It came out on a low, dangerous growl, reminding Rachel of one of his former code names: *Panther.* At the time she hadn't realized exactly how well that alias had fit.

Reminding herself that she had nothing to fear from this man, she said, "That policeman over at the other table, the one who came in just a minute ago, is watching us with increasing interest."

Although he didn't move a muscle, Rachel was aware of Shade's surreptitious sideways glance. "I would suggest," she continued calmly, "if you wish to avoid spending the remainder of the evening down at the precinct house responding to questions you'd rather not answer, that you leave your weapon safely where it is."

Damn. He hadn't even noticed the cop come in. No doubt about it. He must be getting soft in his old age.

That unsavory idea reminded him of an old intelligence agency bromide: There were old spooks and bold spooks, but there were no old, bold spooks. Shade slowly dropped his hand to his side.

"Who the hell are you? And what do you want with me?"

"My name is Rachel Parrish. And I want to accompany you to Yaznovia."

There. It was out in the open. She hadn't broached the subject as tactfully as she'd planned, but then again, tact and patience had never been Rachel's long suit. There were some things that even death couldn't alter.

"You're from the company." Shade wondered why he hadn't figured it out the minute she'd shown up. Obviously the desk jockeys were afraid that, left to his own devices, he'd screw up some unfathomable government foreign policy.

"No. I'm not from the CIA."

"Sure." She was good, Shade admitted as he swiped at the damn fern again. Everything about this woman—her unwavering gaze, her steady expression, her understated appearance, her composure—all screamed sincerity. "That's what they all say."

He still had the scar between his shoulder blades where an unbelievably sexy, redheaded double agent had stabbed him while they were taking a hot shower together in a supposed safe house in the German countryside. Six years later and Shade still hadn't figured out where she'd hidden the damn stiletto.

His intelligent eyes were looking into Rachel. Looking hard. Looking deep. Men had looked at her that way before, while questioning her during her fatal trial. At the time, they'd professed to be merely probing for the truth, but Rachel had understood all too well that they'd already found her guilty.

But this man was not like those others, Rachel reminded herself. Shade was rough-hewn, yes. He'd done things that he would someday have to atone for. But despite his outward cynicism, she knew that he possessed a deep-seated, unflinching integrity. He was also old-fashioned enough to believe in justice.

She'd always seen things in Shade others couldn't see. Things he'd never seen in himself. She also knew that it would irritate and embarrass him to discover that she considered him an unshakably moral man.

Such knowledge allowed her to hold her ground beneath his sharp stare. Although looking into his unwavering eyes was like gazing into a too-hot sun, if he expected her to squirm, he'd be disappointed.

"I understand why you might doubt my word. But I assure you, I'm not a spy."

She was a helluva lot better than good. There weren't many people who could stand up to a look designed to make the bad guys tremble in their boots. Most individuals with something to hide began to fidget. Flush and look away. Sweat. But she remained as cool as a frozen daiquiri.

"I think," he said slowly, determined to get to the bottom of this unexpected twist in plans, "we need to talk."

"Yes." Her pleased smile, now that she'd gotten her way, was nothing less than beatific. It lit up her eyes to a gleaming pewter, softened her features, and for a fleeting instant, he almost remembered where he'd seen her before. And then the illusive image faded.

"But not here," Shade said, as the noise level in the bar rose. The place was becoming packed with people all eager to see and be seen. Music blared nonstop; voices grew progressively louder, the blender whirred incessantly.

"It is a bit clamorous."

Having achieved her first objective—that of making contact with Shade—she was becoming more aware of her surroundings. Accustomed to eternal peace and serenity, Rachel's ears were beginning to ring from the interminable music.

The unfamiliar scents, the crush of people crowded shoulder to shoulder, seemingly unfazed by such physical intimacy, was making her claustrophobic. Her body suddenly felt disturbingly fragile, as if she'd shatter like crystal if anyone so much as brushed against her.

Moisture beaded up on her forehead and above her top lip; her hands grew cold. Tiny spots had begun to swim in front of her eyes.

Not one to miss a thing, Shade noted her sudden distress, along with her valiant attempt to conceal it. She reminded him of some naive little missionary plunked down into a village of cannibals.

He polished off the rest of the Scotch. "You hungry?"

Rachel shook her spinning head to clear it. She took a deep, calming breath, unaware of the way it caused her unfettered breasts to rise and fall provocatively beneath the black wool.

The change of subject momentarily confused her. Then, as if on cue, she felt an unfamiliar rumbling in her stomach. She pressed her palm against the front of her straight skirt, as if to quiet it. "I think I am."

"I skipped lunch today and I'm starving. Wait here while I make a quick call, then we'll leave. We can eat dinner while we talk."

More than a little eager to escape the crowded tavern, Rachel nodded her assent.

After briefly filling Marianne in on what he'd learned so far, and promising to give her more details later this evening, Shade returned to Rachel, who was standing exactly where he'd left her, slender arms wrapped around herself in an unconscious gesture of self-protection.

She had, he saw, retreated somewhere deep inside herself. She was as stiff as a marble statue and her eyes were directed toward the floor, her lashes a sooty fringe on her ashen cheeks.

Sympathy stirred and was immediately and firmly squelched. "Okay. Let's go."

Her relief was so quick and so palpable, Shade felt as if he could have reached out and touched it. Obviously the lady was not as cool and collected as she'd first appeared.

When he put his hand on her back, guiding her expertly through the crush of government employees on the prowl, a bubbly sensation Rachel could not identify rose up inside her.

When she would have stepped away, his hand moved to her arm, holding her so tightly beside him that their bodies were nearly touching. His hard thigh brushed against hers; the brief, unnerving impact almost made Rachel's knees buckle.

"You all right?" Shade felt her sudden stumble, and his grip tightened.

"I'm fine." Rachel groaned inwardly as she realized, despite the very best of intentions, she'd already told her first falsehood. Joshua would be terribly disappointed.

The unpracticed lie was as clear as glass, making Shade all the more suspicious. Who the hell was she? he wondered. And why did she seem so damn familiar?

They didn't talk as they made their way through the combination railroad station/upscale mall. In the distance, a disembodied voice coming from a loudspeaker announced trains leaving for Baltimore, Philadelphia, Boston and New York City.

As the bustling crowds surged around them, Rachel's uneasiness increased. So many people, she thought, moving instinctively closer to Shade. Where were they all going in such a hurry? The unfamiliar crush of humanity made her head begin to swim again and this time she was grateful for his touch as he put a strong, almost protective, arm around her shoulders.

Outside Union Station, a taxi was unloading its passengers. Shade waved it by. Then another. He stopped the third.

"Was there something wrong with those first two?" Rachel asked. Now that they were outside, she found herself able to breathe again. Her mind cleared, allowing her to remember her mission.

"I like this one."

Years ago, he'd been driven around Moscow by a trio of KGB agents who were not exactly thrilled to discover him in their country. Two hours later, he'd learned three important lessons: KGB agents tended to be humorless thugs, broken bones healed and never, ever, take the first cab that conveniently shows up just when you're looking for one.

As he opened the back door for her, Shade glanced with seeming casualness at the cab behind them, making a mental note of the license plate: Able Kilo X-ray 398.

Rachel slid gracefully into the back seat, treating Shade to a flash of thigh. Whoever she was, the lady definitely had world-class legs.

"Feeling better?"

Once again, color rose in a complexion that was a study in winsome pastels. "I'm fine," she said quietly, folding her hands neatly, almost primly, in her lap. "Thank you for asking."

"You looked like you were about to pass out."

"I think it was the heat in the tavern. Now that I've had some fresh air I'm feeling very much better." She smiled. "It was very kind of you to be concerned."

His broad shoulders moved in a careless, irritated shrug. "Lesson number one, Sister Rachel. I'm never kind."

Knowing better but not wanting to engage in an argument, Rachel didn't answer. Instead, she turned her attention toward the passing scenery.

Rachel had never ridden in an automobile. Add to that the chaos that was rush-hour traffic in the District and she found the journey to the restaurant to be a trip she knew she would never forget.

As the taxi driver tore through the streets, Rachel clung to the edge of the cracked vinyl seat. The experience was absolutely terrifying. And exhilarating. Adrenaline, once felt but long ago forgotten, coursed through her veins as the cab careened around a corner.

Behind the cover of the dark glasses he'd donned after leaving the bar, Shade watched her with unwavering interest that he told himself was strictly professional.

Bright color stained her high cheekbones, her lips were slightly parted, she was breathing in short little gasps, and her white-knuckled fingers were grabbing onto the edge of the seat as if she were afraid she was in danger of spinning off the edge of the world. Although there was nothing remotely sensual about the madhouse that was Washington late-afternoon traffic, she looked, Shade mused, exactly like a woman approaching orgasm.

"You must not be from around here," he probed.

She closed her eyes as the taxi abruptly cut in front of a Shoreham hotel curtesy van, earning a deafening squeal of brakes, then a furious bleat of the van's horn.

"I'm not." Now that, she considered, was a major understatement.

Gingerly she peeked again, just in time to watch the driver cut off a delivery van. "Is the restaurant very far?"

"No. So where's home?"

Relief flooded through her. As admittedly thrilling as the ride was, she didn't know how much more of it she could take. "I was born in Massachusetts."

"Ah. I thought I recognized the accent." Although the cadence was different, it reminded Shade slightly of Marianne's Bostonian tones. Perhaps that was why she seemed familiar. "Boston?"

"Salem."

"So, do you live there now?"

"I left some time ago. Dear Lord," she murmured, pressing a palm against her pounding heart as two bicyclists suddenly cut across three lanes of fast-moving traffic.

In the front seat the driver leaned on the horn and shouted a string of colorful, imaginative curses out the open window. The lead bicyclist responded with the raised middle finger of his gloved hand.

"So, where do you live now?"

"Oh, here and there." She wondered what he'd say if she told him the absolute truth, and decided he'd probably take her directly to the local lunatic asylum.

"What do you do? Here and there. For a living," he added at her blank look.

"I'm a midwife," she answered, relieved that the cycle had gone full circle and her former occupation was returning to vogue. Another falsehood safely averted.

"I thought midwives went out with gaslights and horse and buggies."

"They did lose popularity for a time," she agreed. "But now there are a great many women who prefer having their children at home, with their family present."

"Sound like leftover hippies to me," Shade decided.

She tapped down the flare of irritation created by his dismissive attitude. "Well, you're certainly entitled to your opinion. But you're wrong," she was unable to resist tacking on.

"If I'm wrong, why don't you tell me more about your work?" he suggested. "In order to help me better understand?"

He wasn't at all interested in her work as a midwife, Rachel knew. He was digging for information about her. About her past. She wondered if telling him the unvarnished truth would wipe that superior expression off his rugged face.

"Oh, look," she breathed, partly in an attempt to change the subject, partly in heartfelt appreciation of the sight, "aren't the cherry blossoms lovely!" The flowers reminded her of puffy pink clouds.

"Gorgeous." He didn't bother looking at the world-famous trees, decked out in their best springtime finery, bordering the equally famous Tidal Basin. "Have we met?"

Rachel sighed. She'd been waiting for this question. "Met?" she hedged, thinking back on that brief episode when Shade had been trapped under the ice. "No," she said with absolute, unwavering conviction, "we've never met."

Shade had very good instincts about people. More than once his life had depended on such intuition. He sensed she was telling the truth. But he still couldn't quite shake the feeling their paths had crossed before.

"Then why do I feel as if I've known you?"

"Perhaps in some previous life?"

"Sorry, sweetheart, but I don't believe in previous lives, second sight, Ouija boards or any other hocus-pocus kind of stuff." He didn't add that he'd never bought into Santa Claus or the Tooth Fairy, either.

Rachel knew all too well that Shade possessed a relentlessly logical mind. It had been folly to even attempt to throw him off track.

"Well," she murmured with a slight shrug of her shoulders, feigning intense interest in the towering marble and granite obelisk the cab was approaching, "they say everyone has a double."

As they passed the Washington Monument, she thought back to the gallant young revolutionary soldier she'd seen through that freezing winter at Valley Forge. He'd survived the war, with her help, and had gone back to his Virginia farm where he'd married and fathered six children and lived happily ever after with his family for another thirty years.

"That's what they say." But Shade didn't believe he was remembering Rachel Parrish's double any more than he believed they might have been acquaintances in a previous life.

He and Rachel Parrish had known each other. Shade was positive of that.

Now all he had to do was figure out when. And where.

Which shouldn't be all that difficult, he assured himself as the cab pulled up in front of the restaurant. Not with the entire intelligence community at his disposal.

He glanced out the back window to ensure they hadn't been followed. As he exited the cab, Shade decided to get the guys started on the lady's background check right away. Although she seemed harmless enough, it was, he told himself as they entered the restaurant, the prudent, the only, thing to do.

3

THE RESTAURANT, nestled amid the restored Victorian town homes and lush gardens of Georgetown, was an oasis of tranquillity in the teeming, bustling capital city.

The tables were draped in pink damask and had been placed far enough apart to permit intimacy between diners. Candles glowed warmly in crystal holders, Impressionist paintings and gilt-framed mirrors adorned walls covered in silk paper. In a far corner, a tuxedo-clad man played Gershwin on a gleaming black Steinway grand.

"Oh, this is absolutely lovely," Rachel enthused after the maître d' had welcomed Shade back to Washington, led them to a plush banquette at the back of the room, handed them a pair of tasseled menus and the wine book with a continental flourish, then departed.

At first she was surprised Shade had chosen such a pretty location for his interrogation, then recalled his talent for putting his intended victim off guard. A person would not be likely to expect a brutal grilling in these genteel surroundings.

Shade glanced around with a decided lack of interest. "It's okay, I guess." They'd been shown to Shade's usual table. Although a long way from the power booths located at the front of the restaurant, it allowed him to view the entire room while engaging in private conversation. It also kept his back to the wall.

He handed her the leather-bound wine list. "I've got some business to attend to. Why don't you pick out something for us to drink?"

Her attention drawn to what appeared to be either an original Monet or a very good copy hanging on the wall behind him, Rachel nodded absently.

Ignoring the bank of pay phones in the hallway leading to the rest rooms, Shade took the service elevator to the second-floor offices.

The manager of the restaurant, long appreciative of the business Shade and his colleagues represented, greeted him as expansively as the maître d' had, hoped he was enjoying his visit to Washington, then left the office without being asked.

Shade claimed the black leather chair behind the desk, picked up the phone and dialed a number he knew by heart. An unfamiliar, obviously computerized female voice came onto the line, asking for his security code. Missing the flirtatious banter of the old operators, Shade punched in the new five-digit code he'd acquired just that afternoon.

There was a brief pause as the computer verified the number, then a clicking as the call was processed.

On the other end of the line, in an office in suburban Virginia, the phone was picked up on the very first ring.

"McGee," the voice answered.

"It's me." Shade was also not into proper telephone etiquette.

"Christ," Agent Elizabeth Anne McGee complained when she recognized Shade's voice. "It's only been a couple hours since you left here. I told you we'd put a rush on the job, but you know Tony's a perfectionist."

"I'm not calling about the papers. I want you to run a background check on someone."

"Dammit, Shade," she complained, "I was just on my way out. I have a date."

"A date?"

"Yeah, you remember what that is, don't you, lover? A few drinks, a nice dinner in an out-of-the-way bistro. Maybe, if the guy's real lucky and treats me real nice, a little roll in the hay at the end of the evening. A date," she repeated. "Kinda like what you and I used to do, except we never seemed to get around to the dinner."

"I don't remember you ever complaining."

"I wasn't complaining now. I was just pointing out that I had other plans for my evening. With a guy who doesn't flinch every time he sees me slip into my shoulder holster."

"Does he work for the Company?"

"Hell, no." She laughed, but he thought the sound lacked her usual self-assurance. "He's a cardiologist at Georgetown hospital. And he must be a little cracked, because he's actually talking marriage." Another shaky little laugh. "What do you think, Shade? Can you see me as a doctor's wife?"

"You'd make a damn terrific wife, Liz." Shade meant it. Realizing that he'd never be able to give her what she deserved—a home and a family—was the reason he'd let their affair drift away.

This time her laugh held a bit more of its old spunk. "Why don't you write me a reference letter?" she suggested. "Just in case my feminine persuasion needs a little backup."

"I really need this, sweetheart." His voice was low and warm and compelling. Although he did not recognize it as the same tone he used to coax women into his bed—not that they ever needed all that much coaxing—Agent Elizabeth McGee did.

He heard her resigned sigh resonate over the wires. "If I end up an old maid, it'll be on your head," she grumbled. "Shoot. What's the name?"

"Parrish. Rachel Parrish."

"Rachel?" He could practically see her auburn brow climbing her forehead. "If you're using me to prescreen your bed partners these days, Shade—"

"It's strictly business."

"Sure. And I've got some beachfront property in lovely downtown Beirut I'll sell you for a song."

"Liz." His voice dropped into its lowest registers. "Have I ever, in all the years we've known each other, lied to you?"

There was a long pause on the other end of the line. "No, Shade. You were always unflinchingly honest." She actually sounded hurt, which surprised him, since he'd always prided himself on being completely upfront about his aversion to setting up housekeeping. It wasn't that he didn't like women. A steady stream of them had shared the moment, and his bed, since the summer he'd turned fourteen and had been seduced by the orphanage's new nurse, a married, decidedly lusty older woman in her thirties.

Other women had followed. Although sex, he'd discovered that long-ago sun-drenched day, was easily acquired, no woman had ever made an imprint on the dark interior of his spirit.

"You said Parrish?" Her tone was briskly professional.

"Rachel," he confirmed.

There was a tapping of fingernails on computer keys. "Age?"

"I don't know exactly. Mid-twenties. Five foot four, one hundred and five pounds, dark blond hair, gray eyes."

"Aha," Liz murmured, as if he'd just confirmed her previous suspicion. "Where's the lady from?"

"She said she was born in Massachusetts, and I think her accent, if it's not faked, backs her up. But she also hedged when I asked her where she's been living recently."

"No problem. Social Security and tax records will have that." More tap-tap-tapping. "Occupation?"

"Midwife." When he didn't receive the disbelief he'd expected, he added, "She says having kids at home is back in fashion." His voice went up on the end, turning it into a question.

"It is. And not just on those leftover hippie communes in northern California, either."

He laughed at that. "You know me too well, Liz."

"I always did, Shade. Which explains why I gave up on you and decided there was something to be said for cardiology."

Shade couldn't think of anything to say to that. It was, after all, true.

"So, can you give me anything else about this Rachel Parrish?" Elizabeth McGee asked.

"Sorry, that's it."

"Don't worry. If the lady's not in my data banks, she doesn't exist. By tomorrow morning, I'll know her shoe size, the name of her hairdresser, any other jobs she might have had and every guy she's gone to bed with since her senior prom."

Personally, Shade didn't think that last list would be very long. He wondered what Liz would say if he suggested she might want to check any nearby convents for runaway nuns. Or missing vestal virgins.

There was something about Rachel Parrish. Something so—Shade searched for the proper word—*undefiled*. An archaic term, he considered, after it had popped into his mind. But strangely, it fit.

"Mainly I want to know if she's intelligence," he revealed. "And whatever ties she's got to Yaznovia."

There was a moment's silence on the other end of the line.

"Be careful," Elizabeth McGee said finally. "This cockeyed plan of yours is going to be hard enough to pull off without getting involved with Mata Hari."

"Piece of cake," Shade promised. He'd been told his entire life that his plans wouldn't—couldn't—work. Which always made him all the more determined to prove his detractors wrong.

And this time, he thought as he hung up the phone, he could not afford to fail. Because this time, it was personal.

RACHEL STUDIED the wine list, staring at the mind-boggling choices. She was trying to decipher the myriad foreign and American choices, but she might as well have been attempting to read Sanskrit.

"Does *mademoiselle* have a special request?" a deep, all-too-familiar voice inquired, breaking into her concentration.

She glanced up, clearly startled. "Joshua? What are you doing here?"

"Playing the piano. And a very fine instrument it is, too," he commented, flexing his fingers with overt satisfaction. "Did you like my rendition of 'Rhapsody In Blue'?"

"To tell you the truth, I didn't even notice." She glanced nervously around, worried that Shade would return at any minute. "Surely a sudden musical urge didn't bring you all this way."

"Of course not. I came to check on you. How are you?" He leaned close, looking into her eyes, seeing all the way to her soul.

"I'm fine."

"You looked pale in the tavern."

"I just needed a slight period of adjustment. I'm feeling much better now. Really."

He seemed willing to take her words at face value. "Have you deterred Shade from his mission?"

"Not yet. Really, Joshua, these things take time."

It was clearly not the answer he'd been hoping for. He arched a silver patrician brow. "How much time?"

A flare of impatience burned away the last of the cobwebs fogging her mind. "I don't know. Shade is very intransigent. And since I've been forbidden to tell him the truth, I must find some other way to reach him."

"Work quickly," Joshua advised.

Rachel recognized the tone. All too well. She sighed. "You're here to bring me my deadline, aren't you?" When she'd left, that last detail had not yet been agreed upon.

"Yes." His warm gaze offered encouragement, and a warning she knew would be folly to ignore. "You have five days."

"Five days!" Realizing that she'd raised her voice, she quickly glanced around to ensure she hadn't drawn any undue attention. "It will take at least two or three days to even get to Yaznovia."

The brow lifted again, this time higher. "Surely you do not plan to accompany Shade to Yaznovia."

"If it proves necessary, yes." Jittery all over again at the gravity of her mission, Rachel vowed not to fail. "I must do this, Joshua."

"I understand your concerns, but—"

"You must go back and try to win me a little more time," she interrupted earnestly. "Please, Joshua?"

The older man let out a breath on a soft sound. "I'll try, little one." Then he did something he'd never done before. He brushed his knuckles affectionately, lovingly, down her cheek. "Take care, Rachel. I fear that this time your dedication and enthusiasm may have gotten you in over your head."

He lowered his hand. "'Embraceable You,'" he said, raising his voice to a purposefully public volume. "An excellent choice, *mademoiselle*. One of Gershwin's most memorable works. And a personal favorite of mine, as well."

Giving her one last fond yet warning look, he returned to the Steinway.

Leaning her elbows on the table, she linked her fingers together, braced her chin on her joined hands, watched Joshua settle himself theatrically at the piano and willed herself to relax. But the jumpiness in her refused to dissipate.

Her nerves were not helped by Shade's return. He was crossing the room toward her, looking once again, she considered, like a great dark cat.

"Did you choose our wine?" he inquired blandly.

Rachel glanced cautiously up and found herself looking straight into the pagan iridescence of Shade's green eyes. A ripple of fear and something else, something dark and dangerous she could not identify, skimmed up her spine.

"I thought I would prefer to leave that to you." It was only a whisper, forced past the tattered heartbeat lodged in her throat. Rachel took a breath and tried again. "Did you get your business taken care of?" Her smile was frail and false.

"For now."

Shade slid into the booth, cynically enjoying the slight tremor she tried to hide but couldn't when his leg brushed against hers beneath the table.

He hadn't missed the intimate little tête-à-tête between Rachel and the pianist. It only confirmed his suspicions that she was not as innocent as she appeared to be.

Whoever Rachel Parrish was, he wasn't about to let her interfere with his mission. He'd get into Yaznovia, rescue Conlan, kill the general—nice and neat and clean, not the lengthy, drawn-out, messy way the cold-blooded bastard did away with his innocent victims—and most importantly, return Conlan to his pregnant wife.

And if Sister Rachel thought she was going to stop him, Shade thought savagely, the wide-eyed little nun was in for the surprise of her life.

She was good. Better than good, Shade decided more than two hours later. Contrary to her innocent butter-would-melt-in-that-soft-mouth appearance, the woman was proving to be a world-class equivocator.

Along with a sixth sense that allowed him—at least most of the time—to know when people were lying to him, Shade had always prided himself on his ability to cut through the tangle of prevarication and get to the truth.

But Rachel Parrish was putting that well-honed talent to the test. As the meal dragged on, he had grown increasingly frustrated.

Diners at tables all around them finished their meals and left the restaurant; others took their place, then after a time, left, as well. Finally, only Rachel and Shade remained.

"Let's try this one more time," Shade said, after the waiter had taken away their plates, refilled their coffee cups, delivered the two Napoleon brandies Shade had ordered, then discreetly left them alone again. "Why the hell would you—or anyone else for that matter—want to go to Yaznovia?"

Rachel sighed. The strain of her uncustomary physicality and the unrelenting pull of gravity on her body was tiring enough, without Shade having grilled her for hours.

"I've told you—"

"I know." His hand sliced the air. "It's personal."

Rachel nodded. "I'm sorry. But I can't reveal the details. All I can say is that—"

"It's a matter of life or death," he interrupted her again, his deep voice raspy with sarcasm.

"That's right."

"Do you have any idea what's going on over in that hellhole?"

Only too well, she could have answered, remembering how she'd been forced to stand by as Shade had been so brutally tortured. "I know that the country has fallen under the thumb of a ruthless dictator. I know that hundreds, thousands, of Yaznovians have been killed. And many more will die if the general remains in power."

She could have gotten that information from any news broadcast or weekly news magazine. Yet the pain that shadowed those strangely familiar gray eyes suggested that her knowledge of the general's crimes came from a much more personal source.

It crossed his mind that he undoubtedly wasn't the only person in the world who might want to knock off Rutskoya. This woman sure as hell didn't look like an assassin. But, Shade reminded himself, he had the scars to prove that appearances were often deceiving.

"Have you ever even been to Yaznovia?"

"In a way." Attempting to answer his questions without actually lying was getting extremely tiresome for someone who'd spent the past three hundred plus years telling nothing but the truth.

"In a way," he muttered. These half answers were driving him crazy. "What the hell does that mean?"

How could she explain that her spirit had remained with him during those long months of imprisonment? Just as it had all of his life?

What would Shade say, Rachel wondered, if he knew that wherever he'd gone, from the moment he'd drawn his first breath, during all his travels to those dangerous places, she had, in her own way, remained unceasingly by his side.

"I've been to Yaznovia," she said. It was, in a way, the truth.

"Not as a tourist."

"Not exactly."

There she went again. "Not exactly," he repeated. He closed his eyes and prayed for strength. When he opened them again, he gave her a long, hard, uncomfortably probing look.

"I never forget a face," he murmured thoughtfully. "And despite all that New Age garbage about reincarnation or doubles, I know damn well that I've seen yours before."

He was suddenly very close to her. Too close. His eyes, which had reminded her of emeralds earlier, now reminded her of a stormy sea. There was steel beneath his quiet tone, and Rachel could feel the energy radiating from his unnervingly masculine body. Even more disconcerting was the distinctly feminine force she felt awakening deep inside herself.

"Was it in Yaznovia?"

"No."

She was telling the truth, Shade decided. But like everything else about this woman, it wasn't the entire story.

"You say you're not with the CIA," he began again.

"Nor Interpol, or the Mossad, or KGB or any other espionage agency," she confirmed. On this she was definitely on solid ground. "I am not a spy, a counterspy, a double agent or anything else like that."

"If you were a double agent," Shade pointed out, "you'd hardly announce the fact."

"True," she allowed. "I suppose you'll just have to take my word for that."

"Nothing personal, sweetheart, but I'm not in the habit of taking anyone's word for anything. And I damn well wouldn't believe you even if you were to tell me the sky was blue, or the sun rose in the east every morning," Shade snarled.

He felt her flinch. Despite the fact that she'd held up amazingly well during his interrogation, she was looking exhausted, tense and nervous, all at the same time. Shade experienced another momentary pang of guilt and ignored it.

"I'm sorry if I've made you angry."

Her gaze was directed downward at the tablecloth. Her hands, wrapped around the brandy snifter, were unconsciously stroking the crystal sides in a way that created an unexpected surge of heat down his spine.

"Sorry enough to tell me the real reason you want to go to Yaznovia?"

She didn't immediately answer. But the flush of color in her cheeks proclaimed her guilt as surely as if it had been written across her face in bold black script.

She glanced over at the piano, seeking solace from Joshua, but he was not there. She was on her own.

"I can't."

"Can't? Or won't?"

"Please try to understand," she said in a voice just barely above a whisper.

"That's precisely what I'm trying to do, sweetheart." From his gritty tone, Rachel knew he did not mean the term as an endearment. "But you're not exactly a font of information."

Realizing that he wasn't going to relent until she'd given him some excuse, Rachel opted for yet another half-truth. "It's a man."

"A man." That came as a surprise. If there was ever a woman who seemed untouched by a male, it was this one.

"He's in terrible danger."

"So is everyone foolish or unlucky enough to still be living in Yaznovia."

"This is different."

Shade took another long, probing look at her face, his own expression shadowed and unfathomable. "By 'different,' you mean personal."

"Yes." In a purely instinctive feminine gesture, she placed her hand on Shade's arm and looked up at him with earnest eyes. "I must save him."

Her fingers were long and slender, her nails neat and short and unpainted. For some insane reason, Shade couldn't help wondering what her hands would feel like on his bare flesh.

The unwilling desire her innocent touch inspired annoyed the hell out of Shade. He plucked her hand from his sleeve.

Not bothering to conceal his irritation, he tossed down the brandy and signaled the waiter for another.

Feeling as if she were standing on the edge of the smoldering crater of a volcano about to erupt, Rachel decided not to suggest that he'd already had enough to drink for one day. Unaccustomed to alcohol, her own head was beginning to spin from the single glass of wine she'd nursed during the interminably long dinner.

"This man," Shade said after another long swallow, "is he your husband?"

She wasn't wearing a ring, but that didn't necessarily mean she wasn't married. From her ultraconservative clothing, it was possible she belonged to some religious cult that didn't believe in worldly behavior, like wearing jewelry.

"No. I'm not married."

"Divorced?"

"I've never been married." Engaged, perhaps. But that grim little tale had nothing to do with her mission here today. And even if it had, Rachel was not prepared to share one of the more depressing aspects of her too-short life.

Shade's brooding eyes studied her thoughtfully over the rim of his glass. "Your lover?"

She blushed at that one. An intriguing flood of pink colored her cheeks appealingly and once again reminded him of one of Raphael's angels.

"No."

"Your father?"

"No."

"You know," he drawled, "we could keep this up all night until we'd worked our way down to your fifteenth cousin on your uncle Merle's side."

"I don't have an uncle Merle."

"Well, that's one down," he said with a wry twist of his mouth. "Which leaves us with innumerable unnamed relatives yet to go."

"I'm sorry. I cannot be more specific."

If he hadn't been so frustrated, Shade knew he would have found it fascinating that such a soft, acquiescent-looking female could possess such an iron will.

He decided to put the question aside, for now. Once Liz came up with Rachel Parrish's bio, he'd know her entire family tree. Along with, as the agent had pointed out, any lovers, past or present.

"Well, whoever the hell the guy is, you must love him a lot."

"I do," she answered without hesitation.

"Enough to risk your own life?"

"In order to save his? Of course. I would do anything for him," Rachel said with renewed fervor. "Anything at all."

Shade wondered what it would be like to be the recipient of the type of unqualified devotion usually—and in his experience, falsely—attributed to dogs.

He'd had a dog once, for a brief time when he lived in Colombia, posing as an unscrupulous former American Airlines pilot eager for some fast bucks. While Shade was busy infiltrating the infamous cocaine cartel, a huge black-and-brown canine of indistinct parentage attached itself to him.

Against his better judgment, Shade had saved the damn whining beast from a fierce monsoon storm, fed it, bathed it, and even managed to round up some tick dip at the local *farmacia*. Six weeks after that, the ungrateful animal ran away. Later, Shade heard his faithless dog had taken up with a BBC reporter.

Something stirred in Shade's gut. Something that felt uncomfortably like envy.

"If I am on my way to Yaznovia, which I'm not saying I am," he qualified brusquely, "what makes you think I'd agree to drag along some helpless, clinging-vine of a female who'd undoubtedly end up getting us both killed?"

Shade wasn't the only one losing patience. Rachel's own temper was beginning to fray. "That's not a very complimentary description."

"In case you hadn't noticed, sweetheart, I'm not in a very complimentary mood."

"Oh, I noticed all right." She was also noticing, to her dismay, how small and delicate the brandy snifter looked in his strong dark hands. A tingle of something both forbidden and exciting danced across her nerve endings. "And I do wish you'd quit referring to me as sweetheart."

Anger turned her eyes a bright and gleaming silver. Shade found such emotion, simmering so very near her proper little exterior, more than a little intriguing. He wondered idly if Sister Rachel might display such passion in bed. "What would you like me to call you?"

She did her best to glare at him. "I'd like you to call me a taxi."

He surprised her by laughing at that. A deep robust laugh that tugged innumerable and horribly dangerous emotional chords within Rachel.

She'd thought she knew everything about Shade Blackstone. Everything, that is, except the unsettling fact that something about this man compelled her on a deep, primitive level.

"I don't know what the hell you're up to, Sister." Unable to resist the way her pale complexion gleamed like pearls in the candlelight, he ran his knuckles in a slow, sensual sweep up the slanted line of her cheekbone. "But I'm beginning to think I'm going to enjoy figuring out your little scheme."

His smile was thin and humorless. Slowly, without taking his seductive eyes from her wary ones, he traced the outline of her lips with his thumb, creating a ring of exquisite lightning.

Rachel was having so much trouble breathing, she worried that she was literally falling apart. Perhaps, when her superiors heard she'd been audacious enough to ask for more time, they'd simply canceled her quest and called her back.

Perhaps any moment now, she'd find herself seated at her computer, watching Shade as she had for all these years. From a sometimes frustrating but always safe distance.

Shade watched her soft pink lips part, he saw the physical awareness stir in her wide pewter eyes and found himself on the brink of something dangerous.

"Let's blow this joint and move our conversation to somewhere a bit more private. Like your hotel."

"My hotel?"

Despite her scant personal experience with men, Rachel had the uneasy feeling that Shade had a great deal more than mere conversation on his mind. A memory stirred—a misty image of Shade and a female assassin together in the shower.

Rachel wondered what this self-professed loner would say if he knew she'd been the one responsible for that bar of soap on the tile floor. The same soap the woman had slipped on just as she'd slashed downward with the stiletto, causing her to strike bone rather than Shade's more vulnerable flesh.

Shade watched the look of self-satisfaction move fleetingly across her delicate features and wondered at its cause. "Where are you staying?"

"The Mayflower." Rachel had decided it was proof of Joshua's sometime warped sense of humor that he'd booked her into a hotel named after a boatful of Puritans. After her unhappy experience in Salem, Puritans were not exactly her favorite people.

Despite that little double cross in the shower, Shade had always been extremely careful when it came to his relationships with women. He had enough danger and unpredictability in his work life. When it came to taking a female to bed, he preferred predictability. He also insisted on remaining totally in control.

But some deep-seated inner instinct told him that control would be difficult, if not impossible, with this woman. Only a few hours with Sister Rachel and he was in danger of getting himself set up before he even knew what the damn game was.

Shade hadn't lived this long by taking unnecessary chances. And Rachel Parrish, as luscious as she might be, definitely represented one helluva risk. Which meant the lady was off-limits until he could find out who she was and what she was up to.

"That's a pretty pricey joint. And no offense intended, Sister, but you don't look as if you're exactly rolling in dough."

He rubbed his chin, appeared thoughtful for a long minute, then said, as if the thought had just occurred to him, "I'm staying with a friend. I know she wouldn't mind more company. How about we go to the Mayflower, pick up your stuff and you can come home with me?"

It was neither a suggestion nor an invitation, Rachel surmised, but an order. "You don't trust me."

"Not on a bet." He tossed some bills onto the table and stood up, prepared to leave. "But don't take it personally, Sister Rachel," he advised when he saw her downcast expression. "I don't trust anyone."

Which wasn't a surprise, considering the life he'd led, Rachel allowed. But such lifelong cynicism was so very sad. As she left the restaurant with Shade, Rachel vowed that before her time on earth was up, she would teach Shade Blackstone to trust.

4

IF MARIANNE O'DONAHUE was surprised when Shade showed up at her home with a blond female in tow, she possessed enough good manners not to show it. She greeted Rachel warmly, even insisting that her unexpected guest take her own bed.

"Oh, I couldn't put you out of your room that way," Rachel said quickly. She felt embarrassed enough about arriving on this woman's doorstep without an invitation.

"Don't worry about it." Marianne waved Rachel's protest away with a graceful hand. Her nails, like Rachel's, were short and unpolished; unlike Rachel's fingers, a simple gold band gleamed warmly on the fourth finger of her left hand. "The downstairs couch is nearer to a bathroom. Which these days, since I seem to be up all night, is a lot more convenient."

Rachel returned the woman's smile and found herself beginning to relax for the first time since her arrival on earth.

"The first months of a pregnancy are difficult," she allowed. "But it gets better."

"That's what they taught me in medical school," Marianne agreed. "But it's hard to remember that when I'm down on my knees, tossing my cookies into the toilet every morning."

"Ginger tea is quite effective for morning sickness," Rachel offered helpfully.

"Really? I'd love to do something to feel better, but I'm trying to stay away from drugs. How do you fix it?"

"Wait just a damn minute!" Shade snarled, suddenly interrupting the women's conversation. He took a menacing step toward Rachel. "How the hell did you know Marianne's pregnant?"

"Why, that's right," Marianne murmured, turning her own curious gaze toward Rachel. "I only found out for certain myself yesterday."

Pride was a definite burden at times, Rachel moaned inwardly. The very same immodesty regarding her midwife ability that had resulted in her untimely death now was making Shade distrust her all the more.

Pride goeth before the fall, Joshua constantly warned her. Rachel knew from personal experience that he was telling the truth. The problem was that she'd discovered the hard way that it was much easier to quote pithy little axioms than to live by them.

"I am, after all, a midwife," she reminded Shade. "I should be able to tell when a woman's expecting a child."

"You're a midwife?" Marianne's eyes lit up with both professional and personal interest. "How wonderful."

She placed a hand on Rachel's arm. "You must tell me all about your work," she insisted, leading Rachel up the stairs and away from Shade's relentless gaze. "Have you ever considered international relief work? The Rescue the Children Fund can always use experienced midwives. Do you know anything about the organization?"

Shade ground his teeth as he had no choice but to let Rachel escape any further questioning for now. He didn't buy this latest lame explanation any more than he did any of the others she'd tried to hand him earlier.

The woman was up to something. But what the hell was it?

IT WAS LATE. A cold, white quarter moon had risen high in the sky outside the bedroom window. Neighborhood lights had all been turned out; the only sound of life on the street was a tomcat crying a lonely, romantic lament on some nearby fence top.

But there was one house on the block whose residents had not yet gone to sleep. Rachel lay on her back in Marianne and Conlan's double bed, trying to discern the muffled voices drifting up the stairs. She knew that Shade was undoubtedly filling Marianne in on what he'd learned today. She also was beginning to realize how frustrating it was to be without her power.

She was accustomed to knowing everything about Shade: what he ate, what he drank, where he went and what perils he was risking. She even knew about all the women he'd bedded in all the remote corners of the globe. But at this moment, her only knowledge came from what she could observe firsthand. And unfortunately, that wasn't a great deal.

She'd heard the tapping of a portable computer in the guest room earlier, before he'd gone back downstairs to talk with Conlan's wife. Ignoring the little voice in the back of her mind that told her what she was about to do was wrong, she slipped out of bed and padded barefoot down the hall to Shade's room.

Afraid that turning on the light might draw his attention, she made her way to the desk by the window. Fortunately, the glow from a streetlight provided sufficient illumination for her to see that the laptop computer was not all that different from the system she was accustomed to.

She pressed a switch, rewarded by a slight humming noise. Moments later, the screen lit up, casting an eerie green glow over the room.

Before she could begin her search for Shade's entry code, a strong arm circled her waist and long fingers closed over her mouth from behind.

"Don't make a sound," the male voice rasped in her ear. "Or I won't be responsible for the consequences." The hand over her mouth tightened. "Understand?"

The unmistakable cold steel of a knife blade was pressing against her neck. Her heart in her throat, Rachel slowly and silently nodded her acquiescence, making no move to struggle.

"All right. Here's how we're going to do this. You're going to put those larcenous hands on top of your head. Then, and only then, I'll release you. Then you're going to turn around very slowly. And if you so much as utter one word, I'll cut that lovely throat."

Rachel didn't believe Shade would follow through on his threat. But knowing that he'd killed before, she slowly lifted her hands and placed them atop her head.

"Okay," he growled. "Now, let's see how good you are at following the rest of my orders."

She felt the steel band around her loosen. Taking a deep breath that was not quite sufficient to calm the wild hammering of her heart, she slowly, gingerly, turned around.

Although he'd released her, he'd not backed away. He was still standing close to her, too close for comfort, close enough that their thighs were almost touching. Close enough that she had to tilt her head back to look at him. Close enough for her to see clearly the cold fury in Shade's emerald eyes, eyes made even greener by the fluorescent glow of the computer monitor.

Close enough to see—dear Lord!—that he was naked. She'd seen Shade Blackstone without clothes before, of course. But never so up close. So personal. So—she swallowed—unnervingly distracting.

Shade's body was every bit as hard as his nature. There wasn't an ounce of fat anywhere on him.

Shade didn't make a move to cover himself up. He stood there, bold and proud in his spread-leg stance. He was holding the knife at his side, but Rachel knew that his almost negligent attitude was feigned. All it would take would be one false move from her and that knife would be at her throat again.

"You know, Sister Rachel," Shade murmured, his lips twisting into a mocking parody of a smile, "if you were that eager to sleep with me, all you had to do was ask. You didn't have to sneak into my room like some second-story cat burglar.

"That is what you came here for, wasn't it? A little midnight tumble in the sack?" His tone was both arrogant and challenging. As was his gaze.

Shade Blackstone was very good at intimidation. Of course, Rachel allowed, the scar helped. As did his deadly knife.

Shade's mocking eyes took a slow, sensual tour down the slender body clad in a white cotton nightgown. The virginal style—floor-length, with a high, ruffled neckline and long, flowing sleeves—was decidedly unrevealing.

Unless its wearer was standing with her back to a bright yellow streetlight as Rachel currently was.

Shade noted with absent male interest that the reflected glow outlined full, high breasts, a slender waist, pleasantly curving hips and long firm legs.

When his gaze lingered on that faint shadowed triangle between her thighs, he felt a slow aching pull in his groin and wondered idly exactly how far she'd go to fulfill whatever the hell mission had her sneaking into his room in the middle of the night.

The idea of taking the little spy to bed was suddenly infinitely appealing. After he'd searched for hidden weapons, of course.

Since he'd not given her permission to remove them, her hands were still atop her blond head. The position, which he'd had her assume for safety's sake, proved to have an added benefit, lifting her breasts and thrusting them appealingly against the thin cotton bodice of her nightgown.

His fingers clasped around one of her wrists. He felt her pulse treble its beat, but the only sign of her fear was a slight dampening of her palms and a white line around her lush lips.

Oh yes, Shade considered wryly, Rachel Parrish was proving quite an interesting challenge.

"Your pulse is beating like a rabbit's. I wonder if that's from fear." Without taking his gaze from her wary one, he lifted her wrist to his own harshly cut lips. "Or something else."

"Really, Mr. Blackstone, I think...oh!" As he treated the other wrist to a feathery kiss, as well, words momentarily deserted her. A breath she'd been unaware of holding shuddered out.

"You think?" Shade prompted. His hands glided up her sides, stopping just beneath her breasts.

This was not what she'd come to earth for, Rachel reminded herself through the delicious mists clouding her mind. It was vital that she regain some semblance of control.

"I think I should be returning to my room."

One hand toyed with the ribbons at the neckline of her nightgown. The other was brushing against her nipple in a tantalizing way that made her flesh tingle. "Before you get what you came here for?"

"This isn't the reason I came here tonight."

"Isn't it?" Those devilishly clever fingers had slipped inside her now-open gown and were tracing a seductive pattern on her heated flesh.

Rachel heard a distant moan and realized through her swirling senses that it had escaped her own lips. She shook her head.

"No," she insisted on something perilously close to a sob. The sensations she was experiencing were too new. Too raw. "It's not."

She was trembling like a leaf in gale-force winds. As her bemused eyes brimmed with moisture, Shade felt another unwilling tug of sympathy. This time he found her discomfort impossible to resist.

He retied the white satin ribbons. "Go back to your own room, Sister Rachel. We'll talk in the morning."

His fingers, no longer gentle, tightened painfully around her shoulders as he marched her toward the bedroom door, then out into the hallway.

She felt his unblinking, intense gaze on her as she returned to the room next door. It took an effort, but she kept her head high, her spine straight. It was only after she was in the safety of Marianne and Conlan O'Donahue's bedroom, only after she'd closed and locked the door, that Rachel gave in to her distress.

On legs that felt like water, she staggered to the bed and sank down onto the mattress. She closed her eyes and pressed her fingertips against the lids, so tightly that the pressure created a dancing display of spinning, golden lights.

Rachel knew she was lucky to have gotten off so easily. Some men—men without consciences, men of the immoral type Shade so often pretended to be—would not have released her without first taking their pound of female flesh.

She lay in the bed—a double bed, made for two—staring up at the swirls on the plaster ceiling. She could hear Shade in the next room, pacing like a caged tiger. Or a sleek, dangerous panther.

Allowing Shade to touch her in such a forbidden, intimate fashion had been wrong. But it had also been surprisingly exciting. Too exciting.

With a muffled groan, Rachel rolled onto her stomach and pulled the down pillow over her head.

Dear Lord, whatever was she going to do?

THE DAY DAWNED BRIGHT and clear. Unfortunately, the sunny morning did not come close to matching Rachel's depressed mood.

Last night's intimate encounter haunted her as she showered and dressed and worked up her nerve to face Shade again. How on earth was she going to make him understand that although she still intended to accompany him to Yaznovia, she would not, could not, permit such forbidden behavior?

Then again, she tried to assure herself as she checked her reflection in Marianne's dressing table mirror, perhaps once he viewed her in the clear light of day, he would no longer find her appealing. She was, after all, far different from the glamorous women Shade usually preferred to take to his bed.

The dress she was wearing today was a drab shade of brown, every bit as sedate as yesterday's black garb. As she buttoned her long cuffs, Rachel was vaguely surprised that the skin on her wrists hadn't been branded by his hot lips.

Shaking off the evocative, too-perilous memory, she tied her hair back into its neat coil at the nape of her neck. She took another quick glance at herself in the mirror. Her eyes, unhighlighted by any cosmetic magic, seemed oddly different to her today.

She leaned closer, studied her reflection judiciously and groaned as she realized the difference was a certain awareness in their depths that had not been there the last time she looked. Awareness and an undeniable eagerness to see Shade again.

She turned to leave the bedroom, then, on impulse, pinched her cheeks. Hard, until they glowed a healthy pink. Not wanting to consider the implications of such behavior, she followed the enticing scent of coffee down the stairs to the kitchen.

Marianne was sitting at the table, reading the International section of *The Washington Post* and drinking from an earthenware mug. She looked up and smiled when Rachel entered.

"Good morning. Would you like some coffee?"

"Good morning. I think I would, thank you."

Rachel studied the pregnant woman with a professional eye. The first trimester of pregnancy was never easy; from the smudged circles beneath Marianne O'Donahue's eyes and her unhealthy pallor, Rachel discerned that hers was proving exceedingly difficult. Which wasn't a surprise, considering how worried she must be about her husband.

"Don't get up." Rachel poured a cup of the fragrant black beverage from the carafe of the electric coffeemaker, and took a tentative taste of the drink that during her time on earth had been declared a forbidden, sinful drink of infidels.

Later, she recalled, Pope Clement, a convert of the bracing brew, had given coffee official Christian status by actually baptizing it.

"I hope I didn't keep you awake last night," Marianne said. "I couldn't sleep, so I turned on CNN."

Watching for news of her husband on the twenty-four-hour news channel, Rachel supposed. That explained the voices she'd heard downstairs. The voices she thought belonged to Marianne and Shade. Obviously he'd been in bed when she entered his bedroom.

"You didn't disturb me at all." The first sip had burned her tongue. Rachel blew lightly on the coffee and tried again. "This is very good," she said, "but do you think you should be drinking it in your condition?"

"Oh, I always stick to herbal tea." Marianne raised her mug as if to back up her claim. "I've always found coffee too strong for my taste, but Shade likes it thick enough to stand a spoon upright."

"Speaking of Shade," Rachel said with feigned casualness, "has he come down yet?"

"Hours ago. He said he had some business to attend to and would be back in a while." Marianne's soft, shadowed eyes revealed her discomfort with the rest of the message. "He also told me I wasn't to let you out of my sight."

Rachel took another sip, enjoying the way the caffeine surged through her system. "I'm so pleased he trusts me."

Marianne could not miss her dry tone. She folded her hands atop the newspaper. "How much do you know about Shade?"

Rachel shrugged. "Enough."

Marianne studied her thoughtfully. Rachel knew she was censoring her words. "Life hasn't been easy for Shade. It wasn't for Conlan, either. But different people respond to life experiences in different ways."

Rachel sat down in a chair across the table from her hostess. "I know he's had a difficult life. But he certainly doesn't make things very easy."

"No." Marianne smiled at that. "Shade is not an easy man to know. And he would definitely not be an easy man to love."

"I think you've misunderstood our situation."

"Have I?" Marianne gave her another of those fond yet probing looks. "No, I don't think so." She smiled and leaned back in her chair. "Your relationship with Shade is none of my business, Rachel, but you have to understand, he means a lot to me. Next to my husband, there's not a person on earth I love more than Shade Blackstone.

"After all he's been through, he deserves some happiness. And I believe," she said firmly, "he's finally found the woman who can make him happy."

Marianne O'Donahue was so open and so honest, Rachel felt guilty at not being able to tell her the absolute truth about her mission. "I think wringing my neck might make him happy," she allowed instead.

Marianne laughed at that. "To tell you the truth, there have been times I've wanted to do the same to him."

"Nevertheless," Rachel said, wanting to set the well-meaning matchmaker straight, "my association with Shade is purely professional. I merely wish to accompany him to Yaznovia."

"Yaznovia?" Marianne's blue eyes widened with disbelief. "Why on earth would you wish to go there?"

"That's the same question I've been trying to get Sister Rachel to answer." The rough, familiar voice shattered the convivial atmosphere of the homey, sun-filled kitchen.

Both women looked up to see Shade standing in the doorway. The thunderous expression on his face was not encouraging.

Marianne pressed a hand against the front of her gray Georgetown sweatshirt. "Honestly, Shade, if you don't stop sneaking up on me that way, I'm going to have a heart attack. The man," she said in an aside to Rachel, "never makes a sound."

Rachel wasn't about to admit that she'd already discovered that disconcerting skill herself. The hard way.

Shade entered the room on long, determined strides, stalking Rachel as if he were a predator. "If you'll excuse us, Marianne," he said, taking Rachel's mug from her hand and putting it on the table, "Ms. Parrish and I are going to take a drive."

"I'll excuse you, Shade," the other woman said easily, "if you promise that you won't take whatever has you so upset out on Rachel."

Shade could have spent hours relating all the ways the woman in question was the one responsible for his ill temper. But unwilling to upset his best friend's wife any more than she already was, he said, "I promise, I won't lay a hand on her."

"Of course you won't," Marianne agreed. "But I don't want you yelling at her, either."

He wondered idly what Marianne would say if he told her the truth. That he believed that Rachel was somehow mixed up with Conlan's murderous captors.

"Shade." Marianne folded her arms across her chest. "I'm waiting."

Shade ruffled her hair in a fond, fraternal gesture. "Sorry, honey, you know I'd do anything for you, but that's one promise I'm afraid I'm going to have to break."

With that ominous statement ringing in Rachel's ears, he reached down and captured her wrist in a painfully tight grip. His fingers felt like manacles on her skin as he practically yanked her from the chair.

"Move it, lady. Now."

He dragged her from the room, across the small foyer, down the front steps, tossed her unceremoniously into the front seat of his rented sedan and fastened the seat belt across her chest.

Shade was angrier than she'd ever seen him; as he threw his own hard body into the driver's seat, steam was practically coming from his ears.

Knowing that he'd never respect a coward, and irritated by his bad manners, Rachel refused to flinch beneath his killing glare.

"Are you always this out of sorts in the morning?"

Flashing her a savage grin, he leaned toward her and placed his hand deliberately on her breast. "If you want a man to wake up in a good mood, Sister, you shouldn't get him all hot and bothered the night before."

His touch was meant to humiliate rather than to arouse. Even knowing that, Rachel experienced a jolt of physical awareness at the feel of those treacherous long fingers.

"You sent me back to my room."

He grimaced at that. "Don't remind me." He squeezed her flesh, felt her nipple respond beneath the ugly brown serge and cursed. "In fact, I don't want you to say a single goddamn word until we get out of town."

"We're leaving town? Where are we going? To Yaznovia? Does Marianne know?"

His eyes narrowed and glittered with dangerous masculine warning. "I said, shut up."

He pressed a button and she heard the four doors of the car automatically lock. Then he pulled the car away from the curb with a roar of the engine.

5

RACHEL HAD HOPED Shade's anger would abate. Unfortunately, if anything, it seemed to grow hotter and more dangerous as they drove in silence along the traffic-packed George Washington Memorial Parkway leading out of the city.

At first she thought he might be taking her to CIA headquarters, but he passed the exit to McLean without a word. Soon they'd reached the Capital Beltway circling the metropolis.

"Are we going to the airport?" Dulles was nearby.

Instead of answering, he shot her a blistering look. "I said—"

"I know." She sighed her own frustration. "Shut up."

He nodded his satisfaction. "Got it."

Soon they were in the Shenandoah, a place of rushing mountain streams and flowering apple trees and a seemingly endless patchwork of fields and farms spread out on either side of the roadway. As they sped past a family of Mennonites driving their horse and black buggy to market, Rachel wondered if, like her, they found the fast pace of modern life unsettling. Rachel wished she could enjoy the magnificent scenery as they drove through the Blue Ridge Mountains, past Civil War battlefields, and quaint little villages that reminded her faintly of towns from her own time.

But she was too aware of Shade's smoldering anger to relax. What was the matter with the man? For not the first time since her arrival on earth, she wished she knew what he was thinking.

For thirty-five years, she'd observed Shade from afar, watching his every move, reading his every thought. She found it both frustrating and ironic that she could be in such close proximity to the man and not have a clue what was going through his mind.

He turned off the Skyline Drive onto a gravel road that twisted up into the mountains. After a time they came to a high wrought-iron fence. Shade punched a code into a remote control and the gate slowly opened, closing behind them.

The white clapboard house, boasting three chimneys, had been built atop a hill, crowning a vast apple orchard. The trees were in flower, their blossoms looking like puffy white clouds. Instead of a lawn, wildflowers surrounded the house like a brilliant carpet.

"It's lovely," Rachel murmured.

Another remote opened the garage. Shade parked the car and closed the heavy steel door behind them. "We're not here to admire the scenery."

As he climbed out of the car, his leather jacket fell open and Rachel caught sight of a flash of blue steel. Even knowing he would never kill an innocent person, the deadly pistol did nothing to soothe her already anxious nerves.

He went around the front of the car and opened her passenger door. "Get out."

"Since you asked so nicely, I believe I will." She flashed him a falsely sweet smile. "Are you going to tell me what we are doing here?"

"You'll find out soon enough."

Rachel's long sigh was the only outward sign of her building frustration. As they entered the house through the garage door, she cast her eyes upward, seeking divine guidance.

With his fingers curled around her upper arm, he led her without ceremony into a book-filled room. The furniture, leather and oak, could have come from some eighteenth-century gentlemen's club. Hunting prints hung on the wall.

"Sit down." He pushed her into a forest-green chair, then crossed the room to the desk.

"Have you ever thought of getting a dog?"

"A dog?"

"Well, you certainly seem to have the vocabulary down pat. Come. Stay. Sit—"

"Shut up," he reminded her through clenched teeth.

Rachel thought she caught hints of both annoyance and amusement in his gruff tone. "That, too," she agreed.

A crystal decanter rested on the leather desk top. Shade poured a healthy amount of Scotch into an old-fashioned glass.

"Isn't it a bit early in the day to start drinking?"

He shot her another of those fulminating looks he'd perfected over the years. "Worried about me, Sister Rachel?"

As irritating as she found his rude behavior, she could not lie. "Yes."

Shade nearly forgot his anger at her seemingly ingenuous remark. He sipped the liquor, eyeing her over the rim of the glass. He was almost fooled. Almost.

"Who the hell are you?" he asked, just when Rachel didn't think she could stand the thick silence another second.

"I told you, I'm Rachel Parrish."

"Yeah, that's what you said, all right." He took another drink. "From Salem, Massachusetts, right?"

She bobbed her head. "That's right."

"Want to tell me why the hell you don't exist?"

Even though Rachel had been waiting for this, his gritty question made her blood run cold. Things were a great deal easier the last time she came to earth, she considered. Then all she'd had to do was dive into that frozen lake and pull him to shore.

Although she'd known he'd seen her that day, he was too frightened and too young to spend much time wondering who it was who'd saved his life. Later, seeking a rational answer, he'd managed to convince himself that she'd been nothing more than a hallucination.

Rachel folded her hands in her lap in an attempt to stop their trembling. "I don't understand. As you can see, I most certainly exist."

"You don't have a driver's license."

"I don't drive."

"Nor a Social Security number."

"I don't work. At least not for money." She thought about telling him that she worked for love and decided he'd undoubtedly take that all wrong.

"So you're telling me that you're independently rich?"

"I suppose you could say that." Wealthy in love and peace, she tacked on silently, thinking of Joshua and all the others in that calm and halcyon world she'd temporarily left behind.

"Want to tell me why the post office doesn't have any address for you?"

"I don't receive a great deal of mail."

Shade flexed his fingers, giving Rachel the distinct impression that he'd love to put them around her neck. He hadn't been all that surprised when last night's wineglass he'd had tested hadn't resulted in her fingerprints being in any government files. If she hadn't been arrested, or in the military, or had a job that entailed getting a bond, she could go her entire life without having a reason to be fingerprinted.

But the entire country—hell, the world, for that matter—was run by legions of faceless bureaucrats who loved their red tape.

Over the years every American was categorized into myriad categories and assigned numbered identities. Birth certificates, baptismal records, drivers' licenses, Social Security, marriage licenses, divorce papers, health insurance plans, credit cards, mortgages—Big Brother was keeping track of all these things. And more.

But Rachel Parrish, whoever the hell she was, didn't even have a damn library card. Impossible! Shade had yelled at Liz.

To which his former lover had suggested sarcastically that perhaps his mysterious stranger was a Pod Person, or a recent visitor from Saturn.

After instructing Liz to go back to work, and concerned about Marianne's safety, Shade had gone home and gotten Rachel out of his friend's house. Just in case.

He polished off the Scotch, put the glass down and crossed the room on the loose-hipped stride Rachel was beginning to find increasingly disturbing, stopping inches in front of her chair.

"I don't suppose you'd like to tell me who you're working for?"

"I told you, I'm not working for anyone." It was nearly the truth. At least close enough, Rachel decided. Besides, there was always the chance that her superiors would be so busy disciplining her over last night's indiscretion, they might overlook a little white lie. "This is personal."

He leaned down until his cold hard face was a whisper away from hers. "Like worming your way into Marianne's house was personal?" he snarled. "What were you going to do? Take her captive, too?"

"I'd never harm Marianne!"

Her shock appeared genuine, Shade allowed, watching her carefully. But, dammit, there was a helluva lot more to this story than the woman was telling him.

"How about Conlan? Did you have anything to do with his capture?"

"Of course not!"

Her eyes were wide and innocent. Shade was finding them too damn appealing for his own good. "So I guess that leaves me."

"You?"

"Am I your target, Rachel Parrish?"

There was no way she could answer that question safely. If she said no, it would be a lie. If she answered in the affirmative, he'd get the mistaken idea she was a professional assassin, hired to kill him in retribution for some past adventure.

"I've told you, I merely wish to accompany you to Yaznovia. I need to go to the country, you're planning to go there, and I believe that you can provide me with much-needed protection."

He stood up and submitted her to another of those long, probing looks. "That's what this is all about? You want my protection?"

"It would be most appreciated." Another half-truth. Rachel decided that she'd probably lied more in the past eighteen hours than she had in her entire life.

"My services don't come cheap."

"I'm prepared to pay. Whatever it costs." Despite the fact that the sky outside the leaded glass windows was still bright and sunny, Rachel heard the distant rumble of thunder and realized that Joshua had overheard her outrageous statement.

He rubbed his jaw. She was still lying. He knew it, with every fiber of his being. The way Shade saw it, he had two choices. He could cut his losses and walk away now, leaving Rachel Parrish to her own devices.

Or he could pretend to buy her sorry little story, what there was of it.

"Nothing is going to stop me from going to Yaznovia," Rachel said quietly, as if sensing his inner deliberation and wanting to sway his decision. "I'd prefer to go with you, but if you don't agree—" she shrugged "—I intend to travel there myself."

He stared down into her gray eyes, seeking some hidden truth. Her determination was evident in every rigid line of her body.

That was enough for Shade to make his decision. Even if she wasn't intending to infiltrate his mission, she could screw things up just the same. At least this way, he could keep an eye on her until Liz and the rest of his contacts in the intelligence community could find out who the hell she was. And what she was up to.

And if she was an amateur, as she insisted, taking her with him would also keep her from inadvertently stumbling into his plan and blowing it sky-high. "Hell." The last thing Shade needed right now were more complications. And Rachel Parrish, whoever she was, represented one major complication. "All right. You can come with me."

"Oh, thank you!" Her relief was palpable. Her luminous eyes gleamed, her face was wreathed in a warm, honest smile that once again struck some distant chord of memory.

But then it was gone, overwhelmed by his lingering frustration. Shade was irritated when he couldn't pinpoint the distant recollection. "But you'll have to play your little game by my rules."

Rachel bobbed her head agreeably. Although she hated to admit it, she'd been worried that Shade was going to turn her down. Not that his refusal would have kept her from saving him, of course. It just would have made her mission far more difficult.

"I understand."

"No, I don't think you do." He scowled as he took in her dress. "Where the hell do you buy your clothes? Missionaries R Us?"

She ran her palm down her wren-brown dress. The shapeless, calf-length garment had a demure high neck trimmed in white lace, and snowy white lace cuffs. "What's wrong with my clothing?"

"Nothing. If you happen to be mother superior to an order of missionary nuns. But that dress is definitely not mistress material."

"Mistress material?"

"I'm getting into Yaznovia as an illegal arms dealer. Your role, Sister Rachel, will be that of my assistant." He flashed her a blatantly sexual smile. "And lover."

"You actually expect me to pretend to be your lover?"

Never, in her wildest dreams, had she considered such a scenario. And she knew if Joshua or her superiors had anticipated such an outrageous outcome, she never would have been granted permission to return to earth in the first place.

"How much you pretend is up to you," he said with a nonchalant shrug, as if only academically interested in the question. "Although it might make things more believable if we really are sleeping together."

She deeply resented the way that outrageous suggestion, tossed so casually at her, made her pulse dance. She remembered last night, how his body felt pressed against hers, hot and hard and so perilously tempting.

"I'm not going to sleep with you."

"That's all right by me." His anger was gone, replaced by that lazy male sexuality Rachel found far more threatening. "When I do take you to bed, sweetheart," he said, rocking back on his heels, "I don't intend to waste time sleeping."

This had to stop! Rachel jumped up from the chair. She was losing her already tenuous hold on her simmering impatience.

"Has anyone ever told you that you are a very annoying man?"

He flung a dark hand against his chest. "Sister Rachel, you wound me."

He was laughing at her! Her eyes narrowed, her face paled with anger. Her fatal temper flared.

"You are," she snapped, poking her finger against the front of his shirt, "the most arrogant, egotistical—"

"You can save the flattery, sweetheart." He caught the stabbing finger and lifted her hand to his lips. "For later."

Rachel tugged viciously, trying to free herself. He ignored her futile gesture and planted a kiss against the sensitive flesh of her palm. And then, turning his back on his lingering uneasiness, putting aside his deep-seated instinct for self-preservation, Shade pulled her into his arms.

Forbidden excitement surged through Rachel's veins. She knew, without a single doubt, that Joshua would be appalled by her unseemly behavior. In truth, Rachel was appalled herself. But her common sense, along with her resolve, had deserted her.

At the first touch of Shade's lips, her mind emptied.

Rachel could taste the remnants of Shade's anger. She could taste his irritating laughter. But most of all, she tasted need. A thick, hot need that echoed her own unwilling desire.

His little spy tasted as good as he'd known she would. Lord, she was sweet. And soft. Her lips were warm and avid, although strangely inexperienced.

She was kissing him back with such fervor that their teeth clinked, but he could sense her curiosity, her uncertainty. "Open your mouth for me, Sister Rachel." His thumb tugged gently downward on her chin.

She did as instructed. When Shade's tongue slid seductively between her parted lips, she let out a soft cry.

Rachel had no idea that men and women kissed in such a manner. At first, she felt self-conscious and awkward for allowing such intimacy. She remained still, accepting the tender invasion, offering him the sweetness he craved.

Gradually the kiss became deeper. And hotter. The sensations were disorienting, worlds different from anything Rachel had ever experienced before.

Shade's bold tongue plunged then retreated, then plunged again, taking what his aching body craved. His arousal was hard against her belly and each time his raiding tongue dove deeply into her mouth, he pushed against her, creating a firestorm within her awakening flesh.

Her whimper of longing was nearly drowned out by his own groan of need. She twined her arms tightly around his neck; her tongue mated with his, at first tentatively, then with a burning passion that equaled the flames blazing like wildfire inside her.

Her straining breasts were flattened by his chest; a thick, aching heaviness had settled between her thighs. In an instinctive attempt to ease it, she pressed against him, unaware that her hips had begun to move erotically against his tumescent flesh.

Shade was used to having his body burn in response to a woman. He was accustomed to a woman's touch making his blood hot and he knew the ability of a woman's mouth to fog his mind. But this was different.

Never had Shade experienced such passion from a mere kiss. The more he drank, the more he wanted. Lord, he couldn't get enough of her. Never had he wanted a woman more than he wanted Rachel Parrish at that moment. He wanted her with an intensity that bordered terrifyingly on need.

Which was why he forced himself to pull back.

Silence descended. It took Shade a full minute to control himself. It took Rachel even longer.

Her breathing was ragged, her senses were reeling. She was shaken. And ashamed. She could not believe she'd responded to him in such a wanton fashion!

In a regrettable display of distressingly feminine pride, Rachel had wanted Shade to find her desirable. She'd wanted him to react to her as an attractive, alluring woman rather than some colorless, celibate nun. She had wanted him to respond to her like a man to a woman.

And he had. The unfortunate problem was that she'd gotten far more than she had wished for. Because Shade had responded with more passion than she ever could have dreamed possible. Kissing Shade had been like riding astride a wild tiger: thrilling and dangerous all at the same time. It was a ride she knew she was going to have to pay dearly for, a ride she must never dare take again.

Shade was studying her, his expression shadowed and brooding.

"You're just full of surprises, aren't you, Sister Rachel?"

"As are you, Mr. Blackstone," she murmured.

"Sounds like we might just be a match made in heaven, Sister."

Her ravished lips curved in a faint, secretive smile. "Perhaps we are."

Despite the fact that Shade was standing too close, despite the fact that her body was still racked with feelings she could not understand, Rachel was almost beginning to relax.

She should have known that the congenial moment couldn't last.

"Or hell," he taunted.

The brief truce was over; the old Shade was back.

"Did you kiss me in order to make me talk?" she demanded.

He surprised her by laughing at that. "Actually I'd prefer you didn't talk. At least not while I'm kissing you. It should have been more than apparent, Sister Rachel, that I kissed you because I want to. And because no matter what you say, you wanted to kiss me, too."

"Heaven help me, I did." She was gazing up at him with regretful fascination.

"I told you, heaven doesn't have a damn thing to do with what's going on here, sweetheart." His fingers cupped her chin, tilting her head to his liking.

Even as she told herself it was wicked, Rachel made no attempt to move away. Instead, she stood still. Waiting.

And then he was kissing her again.

Every nerve ending in his body had narrowed down to his lips, to the ultrasensitive tip of his tongue. The unfamiliar, amazingly erotic sensation fascinated him.

Heaven. He took his time, drinking from Rachel's lips with a slow, lingering pleasure that made it seem as if time had stopped, just for him. For them. Shade savored Rachel's sweet taste and, for the first time in his rocky life, found himself almost believing in the mythical nirvana.

Not only did she resemble an ethereal angel who'd stepped into his life from the ceiling of some medieval cathedral, she kissed like one, too. Her lips, which had revealed her inexperience, now moved on his with a silky, sensual skill.

The kiss was more than a meeting of lips and teeth and tongue, it was a mating of minds. Of hearts. Of souls.

As he drew her closer, sinking deeper and deeper into the prolonged kiss, Shade felt as if he'd waited his entire life for this suspended moment in time. For this woman.

Rachel's mind was clouded with a gilt-edged haze, her resolve, her innocence, her mission, all were forgotten as she felt herself drowning in his warmth, his taste, his scent. Her fingers clutched at his shirt; she arched against him, needing, demanding more.

Another moment of this and Shade knew he'd be lost. Seducing Rachel would not be all that difficult. Hell, if the way she was moving that lush little body against his was any indication, it would be a piece of cake. All it would take would be a little kiss here, a lingering touch there, and she'd be his. At least for the afternoon.

As his aroused body screamed for relief, Shade contemplated going for it.

But common sense, along with a strong self-survival instinct that had kept him alive against all odds during his turbulent, dangerous lifetime, reminded him that it was imperative that Rachel surrender not only her body but her will, as well.

She was still lying to him, dammit. She was still keeping secrets. Secrets that could prove fatal.

So, as difficult as it was, his mind forced his body to forgo what could only be a partial, temporary victory.

When he attempted to end the kiss, Rachel whimpered a faint protest. The soft sound caused his lower body to press painfully against the unyielding zipper of his jeans.

With a self-control that surprised even him, Shade managed to back away yet again from temptation. Both literally and physically.

Rachel stared up at him, her unguarded heart shining in her eyes. If she was faking, Shade considered, the woman was wasting her time playing spy versus spy. Because anyone with that much acting talent definitely belonged in Hollywood.

"Later," he said, his voice roughened with unsatiated need. Unable to resist the silent appeal of those lustrous pewter eyes, he ran the back of his hand down her face and was rewarded by her tremor of lingering desire.

"There can't be a later."

Caught up in his own regret, Shade didn't find her wording peculiar. Later, when his body had cooled and his mind had cleared, he wondered why she had chosen the word *can't* rather than the more decisive *won't*.

"Now that's where you're wrong, Sister Rachel." He traced her bruised lips with a slow, lazy, arrogant thumb. "There most certainly will be a later. And believe me, sweetheart, it's going to be well worth the wait."

Still shaken, Rachel decided that it was time—past time—to make herself perfectly clear regarding her unwillingness to become yet another of Shade's conquests.

"If we're going to be traveling together, we must set some rules."

"We already have rules, remember?" He couldn't resist reaching up to play with a tendril of hair that had sprung loose of its pins. "My rules."

While he absently played with the honey curl, his dark eyes took another slow tour of her now taut body. "You're about an eight."

"An eight?"

"Don't worry, I'm not rating you. If I were, you'd be at least a twelve on a ten-point scale."

Those chauvinistic words should not have given her so much pleasure. But heaven help her, they did. Rachel felt the color rise in her cheeks and wished she could stop this embarrassing habit of blushing.

"I was referring to your dress size. You're an eight, right?"

"Oh."

She had no idea. How was she to explain that the concept of ready-to-wear had not yet been conceived in her day. As for the dresses she was wearing on this trip, Joshua had arranged to have them waiting for her in her hotel room.

Rachel belatedly realized that Shade was waiting for an answer.

Deciding that there was probably no more knowledgeable expert on female bodies than Shade Blackstone, she said, "An eight should be fine."

He nodded his satisfaction. "I thought so." She watched as he picked up the phone and dialed. "Hi, it's me," he said when the voice on the other end of the line answered. "I need some clothes. No, not for me, this is for a woman."

He held the phone away from his ear for a minute. "Come on, Liz," he protested, "I told you, this is strictly business. Size eight. The sexier the better." He grinned. "Ouch. Is that any way for a future doctor's wife to talk?"

His voice was warm and friendly and intimate. It was also missing the gritty edge she was accustomed to hearing whenever he talked to her.

Experiencing an unsettling stab of something that felt like jealousy, Rachel turned away and began to pretend interest in the leather-bound books lining the library shelves.

"I'll need some ID, too. I told you, she's a midwife. No, wait a minute," Shade corrected on second thought. "That sounds too respectable. It's also too dangerous, considering how the general feels about foreign medical people operating in his little fiefdom."

He rubbed his jaw thoughtfully. "How about administrative assistant? That's the kind of ambiguous term that can mean just about anything."

He fell silent again, making Rachel wish she could hear the other side of the conversation. For a woman accustomed to being able to view the entire world—at least the part she was responsible for—Rachel was finding her limited knowledge of what was going on around her increasingly frustrating.

"That's my girl," Shade wound up the conversation. "Thanks, sweetheart. I owe you one." He replaced the receiver in its cradle. "Your new wardrobe will be delivered by dinner."

"I'm so pleased."

Her short tone earned only a shrug. "You wanted to go to Yaznovia, sweetheart. Well, now you're going."

"By your rules."

She picked up a round black marble paperweight from its antique brass holder atop the desk and, for a rash, fleeting moment, actually considered throwing it at Shade's frustratingly arrogant head. With effort, she managed to constrain herself to merely passing it from hand to hand.

He nodded. His eyes turned hard. "Always." The single word, spoken so quietly, and with such repressed violence, was, Rachel knew all too well, a warning.

6

RACHEL SPENT THE DAY alone in the house. After warning her not to leave, Shade had left, declaring that he had things to do.

Although she could not admit it, his rash display of independent behavior terrified her. As she watched him drive away, back down the hill, she realized that for the first time in his life, Shade was truly alone. And all she could do was pray that he'd be safe.

Ignoring Shade's warning about the house being wired, at first Rachel considered risking his fury by going after him. But she quickly discovered that not only were all doors and windows wired with alarms, they were also locked in a way that not only kept intruders out but imprisoned any occupants of the house, as well. Unfortunately, the constraints of her mortal body prevented her from escaping such man-made technology.

Concerned for Shade's safety, she was nearly as nervous as she'd been during her trial. Such tenseness made her grow more and more irritated as time passed.

"It would serve him right if he got into an automobile accident on his way back to the city."

The words were no sooner out of her mouth than Rachel regretted them. "I'm so sorry. I didn't mean that," she said with a quick, pleading gaze heavenward.

As the hours dragged on, her nerves became more and more ragged. She tried to read, but after spending more than thirty minutes turned to the first page of *Gone With The Wind*, she put the thick novel down and turned on the television, hoping for some diversion.

Unfortunately, the afternoon soap operas were decidedly steamy, reminding Rachel all too vividly of the way she felt when Shade kissed her. She watched, fascinated for a few minutes, but when she began to yearn for Shade's forbidden touch, she changed to the movie channel which was playing *Three Days of the Condor*.

Unfortunately, the spy story hit also too close to home for comfort, so she changed the channel again, only to find the equally nerve-racking *Marathon Man*.

When yet a third choice revealed *Mad Max*, Rachel gave up on diversion and returned to pacing.

Finally, just when she thought she couldn't stand the suspense any longer, she heard Shade's car returning up the hill. Relief flooded over Rachel in waves. He was safe! Although it took a mighty effort, she resisted running to greet him. She refused to give him the satisfaction of knowing that he possessed the power to upset her.

He found her in the library, her nose stuck in a book. The late-afternoon sun was shining on her blond hair in a way that made the warm honey color gleam like gold. Once again he wondered idly what it would look like loosened from its prim bun.

"Did you have an enjoyable day?" he asked.

"Delightful." Her tone was rigidly polite as she put aside the leather-bound copy of *Huckleberry Finn*. "And you?"

Shade looked at her with amused annoyance. She was cocky. He'd definitely give her that.

"I got some things accomplished. Oh, I stopped by the house and picked up some stuff you might need. Toothbrush, toothpaste, that sort of thing."

He'd left her clothes behind with the suggestion that Marianne burn them. When Con's wife suggested giving them to charity instead, he'd argued that Rachel's drab dresses were ugly enough to send the average homeless woman into even deeper despair.

"Thank you."

"You're welcome." They could have been taking part in a Miss Manners seminar. Although Shade was surprised to admit it, he decided he actually preferred Rachel when she was arguing with him. "Marianne sends her regards." She'd also warned him to be nice to Rachel, but Shade decided against telling the entire truth. After all, it wasn't as if Sister Rachel had been totally honest with him.

"How is she?" Honest concern flickered in her gaze.

"Holding up as well as can be expected. Oh, by the way, she wanted me to tell you that the ginger tea worked wonders."

"I'm so glad." Rachel's uncensored smile was echoed in her eyes.

Shade was already bored with this genteel, stiff conversation. "You should do that more often."

"What?"

"Smile. You're really quite lovely when you smile, Sister Rachel."

Her palms were damp again. As Rachel resisted the urge to wipe them on her skirt, she felt the embarrassing color rise in her cheeks and she lowered her gaze.

An expectant silence settled over the room. Shade tried to remember when he was last with a woman capable of blushing and realized he'd *never* been with a woman that innocent.

That thought led to another. He wondered how it was, that although Rachel was the exact opposite of his usual women, all he could think about was taking her to bed.

She was surprisingly attractive when she smiled, Shade considered. Despite the fact that she was decked out like some pale little sparrow, beneath the ugly camouflage he could see the possible makings of, if not a great beauty, a very appealing female.

Although she refused to meet his eyes, awareness hummed between them.

Just when she thought she couldn't take the provocative silence another second, the phone on the desk rang, shattering the expectant mood.

"Saved by the bell," Shade muttered, revealing himself to have been no less affected. He was already angry with himself for agreeing to let her tag along on what was bound to be a very dangerous mission.

The call turned out to be from a car phone at the gate. After working his way though what Rachel found to be an incomprehensible series of code words, Shade pressed the button that would allow the delivery van access to the house.

"Wait here," he instructed her in a gruff, no-nonsense tone.

She was becoming accustomed to the way Shade could switch gears without so much as a blink of those devastatingly dangerous green eyes. One minute he was a seductive lover; the next minute she was face-to-face with the grim professional who'd killed before. And who would, if necessary, kill again.

And if his stony expression wasn't enough to convince her that this was not a man to fool with, the gun he pulled from beneath his jacket definitely was.

He returned moments later, his arms filled with boxes, all bearing the name of a trendy Washington, D.C., boutique. "Go upstairs and try these on while I start dinner. There should be some makeup in there, too. Use it."

She stood where she was, not making a move to take the packages. "Don't you ever say please?"

"Not if I can help it." His eyes narrowed. "My rules, remember?" he said on a low, silky tone thick with menace.

"How could I forget," Rachel snapped. Her eyes were shooting little silver darts. "Since you're always reminding me." She snatched the boxes and shopping bags away from him and, with a haughty toss of her head, marched from the library. Shade leaned nonchalantly against the doorframe and watched her stomp up the stairs. Despite her innocent exterior, she was incredibly strong willed. Rachel Parrish was the type of woman who could run roughshod over the most patient, easygoing of men.

Fortunately, Shade had never considered himself either easygoing or patient.

Rachel tried on the various items of clothing, and managed with limited success, following the instructions some helpful saleswoman had colored onto a sketch of a woman's face on a piece of white paper, to apply the contents of several small black-and-gold boxes and bottles. She stood in front of the full-length mirror, staring at her reflection, desperately trying to recognize the unfamiliar woman.

She couldn't do it!

There was absolutely no way she could go out in public looking like this. Indeed, in her day, she would have been stoned for dressing in such an indecent manner in the privacy of her own bedroom.

She was simply going to have to make Shade understand that this was one time he was not going to get his way.

What the hell was she doing up there? Shade glared at the clock for the sixth time in as many minutes. She'd been upstairs long enough to try on Princess Di's entire wardrobe.

Suddenly worried that she may have actually found some way to escape, he took the stairs two at a time, coming to an abrupt halt in front of the bedroom door.

Did he say that beneath the camouflage of those ugly dresses he'd sensed an appealingly attractive woman? He'd been wrong. Incredibly wrong.

Because Rachel Parrish was not merely attractive. She was beautiful. She was stunning. Hell, more than stunning, he realized, the woman was drop-dead gorgeous.

She was clad in a scandalously short strapless black lace dress that hugged every lush feminine curve. It would make any red-blooded male all too aware of the fact that she was wearing little underneath it but perfumed and powdered female.

Her legs, clad in sheer black hose, seemed to go all the way up to her neck. They were also designed solely to make a man sweat. Her bare shoulders were as pale as snow, as luminous as moonlight.

Her breasts, displayed disconcertingly in that plunging bit of ebony lace, reminded him of movie stars of old. Back in the days when glamour and sex appeal were what counted. Lana Turner, Jayne Mansfield, Kim Novak and the incomparable Marilyn.

If Rachel had come into womanhood during the fifties, Shade decided, she would have immediately been declared a goddess.

"Hugh Hefner, eat your hedonistic old heart out."

Rachel didn't need to understand Shade's words to discern his meaning. Looking into his gleaming eyes created a sparkling, bubbly sensation inside her. She ran her hands down the embarrassingly short skirt. "I can't possibly wear this dress."

Her lips had been painted as scarlet as sin and glossed to a wet sheen that made him want to taste her all over again.

"The hell you can't. It fits like it was designed with you in mind."

"It's too revealing."

"That's the idea."

"And these shoes." She frowned down at the skyscraper-high black silk high heels. She'd never worn such unstable, impractical footwear. "I'll never be able to walk in them."

"Don't worry." His lips curved. "I'll hold you up."

She backed away, seeing him approach with seduction on his mind and in his eyes. "Shade—"

"Your blush is uneven."

He picked up one of the sterling-handled brushes, dipped it into the gold compact and, with a quick, expert touch, applied a sweep of rosy color up the slanted line of her cheekbone.

He leaned back, observing his handiwork. "Better." Another soft touch at her temple. "There, see?"

He took her shoulders and turned her back toward the mirror. He was, as usual, right. He was also far too experienced in such feminine skills. How many times had he lounged in bed after a night of making love and watched a woman apply her makeup? Too many times, Rachel warned herself.

"You're very clever."

"And you are incredibly lovely." Standing behind her, Shade held her gaze in the mirror as he trailed a finger over her shoulder, pleased to discover that her flesh was as soft and silky as it looked. "A luscious study in contrasts."

The hell with caution. Shade wanted Rachel Parrish. And he intended to have her. Now.

As it had last night, that thrilling, treacherous hand moved slowly down her neck. "With your proper little manners and your body built for sin."

"Please, Shade—"

"Shh." Unlike his earlier orders, there was no harshness in his voice. Instead, the deep tones swirled around her like ebony smoke.

"So many intriguing contrasts," he murmured. His fingertips were trailing dancing sparks across her warming flesh. "Your jet-black dress. Your snow-white skin." He bent his head and pressed his lips against the flesh his hands had warmed. "Your ruby lips."

Their eyes met in the glass again—his dark and dangerous, hers soft and slumberous. "When I first saw you, you reminded me of an angel from some Renaissance painting or gilt cathedral ceiling.

"But I was wrong. You're not an angel." He turned her in his arms. "You're a witch."

His lips were a whisper from hers. She could feel their heat. "There was a time, my sweet witch, when you would have been burned at the stake for looking the way you do tonight."

His words, chosen for seduction, had the exact opposite effect. Memories flooded back. Excruciatingly painful, fatal memories that turned her heated flesh to cold marble.

She was freezing. A cold wind whipped through her, chilling her all the way to the bone. Smoke from burning torches filled her nostrils and made her eyes tear.

She was standing atop a hill overlooking Salem, surrounded by her neighbors, people who, before the horrors had begun, had been her friends. Sheets of sulphurous summer lightning flashed on the horizon.

Rachel could hear the steady droning of the prayers. She could feel the weight of the rope tighten around her neck. And then . . .

Shade felt her stiffen. She shook her head, scattering pins across the oak plank floor.

"Rachel?"

She was trembling, but not, Shade discerned, from desire. He tipped her head back with a fingertip to her chin. Her complexion was the unhealthy pallor of cold ashes.

Her eyes, rimmed with an attractively smudged line of charcoal, were wide and unfocused. They were looking beyond him, somewhere far beyond his reach. And in their depths Shade saw something that could only be described as terror.

Shade had seen many things in his life. But he'd never seen anyone as terrified as Rachel was now. And he'd never felt living flesh as cold as hers.

"Dammit, what's the matter?" He ran his palms up and down her icy bare arms, attempting to soothe rather than arouse.

Rachel closed her eyes, squeezing her lids as hard as she could, struggling to regain control.

Fighting to remember where she was. And why.

Bit by bit, the past faded away; reality gradually returned.

"Rachel?" Shade watched the awareness rising in her eyes as she slowly, tentatively focused on his face.

"Shade?"

Her ragged whisper, her soft, vulnerable gaze, tore at something elemental deep inside Shade. Something that was far more primal, worlds more dangerous than mere sexual hunger.

He put aside his suspicion. For now. For Rachel. "I'm right here."

He ran his hand down her hair, which, freed of its pins, tumbled over her bare shoulders, gleaming like winter wheat beneath a benevolent sun. His same hand, which could so expertly stroke a woman to climax, now seemed to Shade frustratingly large and clumsy.

"I have to . . ." She looked around, still disoriented. "I need to . . . I have to go . . ." Her mind was as empty as a child's slate on the first day of school; her voice drifted off on a soft, shimmering little sigh.

"You don't have to do anything." He pressed his lips against the top of her head. "You don't have to go anywhere." His arms circled her trembling shoulders.

She straightened, shook her head and gave him a small, fragile smile. "I'm sorry."

As he looked down into her glittering eyes, Shade realized that Rachel had unwittingly discovered a weakness even he had not known he possessed.

He'd wanted her nearly from the beginning. He would not apologize for that. He was, after all, a healthy, thirty-five-year-old male with a strong sex drive. And even in her sober little nun's garb, Rachel was a desirable woman.

If he were to be perfectly honest with himself, he'd admit that the fact the lady represented a danger that could prove fatal if he wasn't careful only added to her appeal.

Shade had, after all, always enjoyed playing with fire. The trick, he'd learned, was not to get burned.

With that end in mind, he'd steeled himself against allowing himself to trust her. What Shade hadn't suspected was that it would be Rachel's unexpected vulnerability that would prove his downfall.

"I'm sorry," she repeated. Her voice was thin and frail. "I feel so foolish."

"I don't need an apology. But I think an explanation might be in order."

What could she say? That his words, meant merely as a compliment, had brought back the darkest moment of her life? That they'd forced her to relive, for the first time in all these centuries, the horrifying details of her death?

Once again it crossed her mind that if she did dare to tell Shade the absolute truth, he'd undoubtedly lock her away in the local asylum.

"It was just a dream."

"You were wide-awake. At least in the beginning." He couldn't vouch for where she'd gone after the tremors had taken hold.

"You've never heard of daydreams?"

His eyes narrowed with the intrinsic skepticism she'd come to expect from him. "I thought daydreams were supposed to be pleasant."

She shrugged. "They can be. But sometimes they're bad dreams. More like nightmares."

He wasn't buying it. Not for a second. But although her flesh no longer felt like ice and her eyes had regained a bit of their spark, Shade reluctantly decided she was still too pale and too shaken to argue the point right now.

"Did Liz happen to toss in any casual clothes along with the femme fatale stuff?"

"Yes." She did not add that she'd been forced to lie on her back on the bed to fasten the embarrassingly snug jeans.

"Terrific." He traced her lips with his finger, tugging the corners of her vermilion-tinted lips up into a semi-smile. "As delectable as you look in this dress, I think it might be a good idea if you change. And wash your face. Then we'll take a walk before dinner."

"A walk?" She glanced over toward the window. While she'd been trapped in the treacherous past, the sun had sunk into the tops of the spring green trees, turning the sky a brilliant gold, then amethyst, then gray. The bedroom was currently draped in dark purple shadows. "Won't it be dark soon?"

"Soon. But there's still time to walk down to the lake. It's a popular place at twilight. If we're lucky, we'll see some deer. Or maybe a beaver or two."

A walk in the brisk spring evening air was just what she needed, Rachel decided. It would clear her head, brush away any lingering cobwebs.

"I'd like that."

"Good." Reluctant to release her, he nevertheless backed away.

In the beginning, the plan had been simple. Get into Yaznovia on his false papers, break Conlan out of prison, slice that murderous dictator's throat, return Conlan to his pregnant wife, then go back to his new home and watch the jungle of weeds grow.

But now, looking down at this unfathomable woman who was part angel, part witch, Shade knew that the next few days could prove to be the most difficult, not to mention the most dangerous, of his life.

7

TO RACHEL'S RELIEF, Shade didn't mention her humiliating loss of emotional control again. Nor, surprisingly, did he resume his seduction attempts.

Indeed, if she hadn't been able to remember every exquisite detail of his heated kisses, of his touch, she might have thought she'd imagined the entire thing.

Over the next three days an unspoken truce was forged. As they waited for their false papers and Shade fine-tuned his plan to get them into Yaznovia, and Conlan out of the country, he was polite, even cordial. But not once did he display the slightest interest in her as a woman.

Rachel told herself she should be grateful that he obviously no longer found her attractive. The problem was, she couldn't lie, not even to herself. Especially to herself.

Each night, as she retired to her room and lay alone in the dark, knowing that Shade was sleeping on the other side of the wall, she thought about how much she looked forward to coming downstairs and sharing a morning cup of coffee with him as they sat on the back porch and watched the sun rise over the tops of the flowering apple trees. How much she enjoyed their surprisingly peaceful evening walks. And, heaven help her, all the hours in between.

And then there was the way she couldn't stop herself from touching him. Always fleetingly. Never sexually. But it was as if her fingertips were constantly tingling with the need to reach out and make contact.

Shade had always meant a great deal to her. Indeed, he'd been the single most important thing in her life for all his thirty-five tempestuous years. The problem was that this time alone with him was forcing her to face some very unnerving truths.

She'd taken personal interest in her charges before; indeed, she'd wept buckets when her Continental soldier had received a near-fatal wound in the battle of Yorktown near the end of the revolutionary war.

She'd mourned again when there was nothing she could do to prevent a silent-film star from tragically drowning in her bathtub on the eve of her wedding. And, of course, children's deaths were always difficult, even knowing that they were destined for a kinder, gentler place.

But her feelings for Shade went beyond mere professional concern. They even surpassed compassion.

The truth was, Rachel admitted on the night before they were to leave for Yaznovia, she loved Shade Blackstone. She had always loved him. In a way that was distressingly mortal.

She also knew that leaving him, as she eventually must, would be the hardest, most painful thing she'd ever done.

Aware of Rachel's intense introspection, and frustrated at his inability to discern what the hell she was thinking, Shade struggled to keep his mind on his mission, even as he fought his increasing attraction to this woman who had become nothing less than an obsession.

Everything about Rachel Parrish fascinated him. He marveled at her serenity, that seemingly innate calm that enabled her to sit quietly for amazingly long periods of time and was such an intriguing contrast to the heated passion he'd already tapped.

He knew how her teeth worried her full bottom lip when she was thinking, he loved the way she absently put her arm through his as they walked down to the pond each night, he was intoxicated by the sound of her laugh, and just the memory of her taste or the silken texture of her porcelain skin was enough to make him hard.

She was a remarkable listener, never interrupting, always making eye contact, constantly touching him in nonsexual, encouraging ways: she'd place her hand fleetingly on his arm, or stroke a feathery fingertip against the back of his hand, or lean forward, her eyes not wavering from his as she brushed a dark lock of hair from his forehead.

Although he wasn't quite sure how she had managed it, she'd gotten him to talk about himself—about his rocky childhood—more during their three days together than he had his entire life. She never pried. She didn't have to, he admitted grimly. All she had to do was to make some casual comment, or ask an offhanded question and pretty soon, before he knew it, he was spilling his guts.

In turn, she frustrated the hell out of him by continuing to refuse to give him any more than the sketchiest information about her reason for going to Yaznovia. He damn well didn't need to hook her up to a lie detector to know that she wasn't telling him the truth.

It wasn't that Shade had any moral constraints about lying. Hell, in his line of work, it came with the territory. Lies, evasions, misrepresentations—all were as common as air.

Whenever he'd question her, she'd calmly look him straight in the eye. And then she'd hedge. Or worse yet, simply answer that she couldn't tell him. Having always prided himself on his ability to separate fact from fiction, he was sick to death of her constant evasions, sick of looking into her lovely face, her remarkable eyes, and knowing that he would not see the truth there.

And if that wasn't bad enough, once he'd let slip his intention to assassinate the general, she'd been after him like a bullterrier with a bone, insisting that if he actually went through with his plan to commit cold-blooded murder, he'd be no better than that despot himself.

And even though he knew that Rachel had a valid point, Shade steadfastly refused to change his mind. The general was going to die. And that, he insisted, was that. Most people, especially those of the female persuasion, were quick to back off when he laid down the law. But it was more than a little apparent that Rachel had never learned the lesson of female acquiescence.

Neither did she seem to possess any feminine guile. Shade waited fatalistically for her to pull out her not inconsiderable womanly wiles in an attempt to convince him to forgo the assassination plot.

By the time they boarded the international flight at Dulles airport, he realized he'd have to wait a very long time for that seduction scenario. Like forever.

The first part of the plan, as Shade had conceived it, involved an overnight stop in the European country of Montacroix, which shared a border with Yaznovia. Fortunately for the peaceful Montacroix citizens, the principality was separated from the warring nation by the Alps.

The royal family, generous supporters of the Rescue the Children Fund, for which Conlan had been working when captured, had offered much-needed financial support to Shade's mission.

"MAY I ASK A QUESTION?" Rachel asked. They were standing at the railing on the deck of a boat that was speeding across Lake Losange, headed toward the palace. "About your plans once we arrive in Yaznovia?"

Shade frowned. Dammit, they'd been over this before. Too many times. "If it's about the general—"

"No." She placed a placating hand on his arm. "It's too lovely a day to get into another argument about that." She said a silent, fervent prayer that she'd still have time to change his mind.

"Actually, I was wondering what you intend to do when the general realizes you're in the country. You're certainly not going to be able to fool him with this false identity."

The name on Shade's forged papers was John Savage. From the murderous expression that darkened his features whenever they talked about the general, Rachel had decided the alias definitely fit. Her own papers bore her real name. When she'd failed to show up in any international police agencies' files, Shade had decided against changing it.

"I don't intend to try to fool the guy," Shade allowed. "You're right. The general and I have had enough run-ins in the past, he'd recognize me immediately." Unless the bastard had tortured so many men they'd all melded together in his criminal mind, Shade tacked on silently.

"So, I'm going to tell him that after I returned stateside with my injuries—"

"Which his men inflicted," she murmured, thinking back on that horrible time when she'd been able to save his life but had lacked the power to prevent his pain. There was a great deal of predestination involved in the business of life, Joshua had reminded her at the time. Sometimes one just had to allow events to take their course.

Damn. Shade regretted having told Rachel about the seemingly endless torture, during one of his uncharacteristic moments of openness. "Yeah. While the general got off by watching."

His jaw hardened at the memory. The general was going to die. And Shade was going to enjoy being the one to send the bastard directly to the lowest circle of hell.

"Anyway, my cover story is going to be that our government had no further use for me. So now, forced to make a living, I had no choice but to turn mercenary. I've also got a lucrative little black-market arms business going on the side."

"Considering the fact that the general is a thoroughly corrupt man, he should accept that story," Rachel agreed.

"In a minute. Especially when I offer him one helluva deal on some ground-to-air missiles recently liberated from one of our German bases. The trick will be getting him to release Conlan as part of the deal."

Rachel knew all too well the reason for the general taking Conlan O'Donahue hostage in the first place. She'd wanted to warn Shade for days, but afraid such knowledge might make him even more suspicious about her intentions, causing him to refuse to let her accompany him to Yaznovia, she'd held her tongue.

Now, having gotten this far, she decided it was time to broach the subject. "Have you considered the possibility," she began carefully, "that the general might be setting a trap for you?"

Shade shrugged. "Sure."

"Aren't you concerned?"

She was an intriguing, sexy, highly intelligent woman. There were also times when she was as transparent as glass. Shade looked down into her troubled eyes, tried to remember the last time anyone other than Conlan or Marianne had worried about him, and came up blank. Her obvious concern moved him in ways he did not want to be moved.

"I've got all the bases covered."

"What does that mean?" Baseball lexicon was not part of Rachel Parrish's world.

Giving in to impulse, and because it had been four very long days and three frustratingly lonely nights since he'd tasted Rachel's sweet lips, Shade bent his head and kissed her. A brief, sweet kiss that nevertheless shook her all the way to her toes.

"It means, don't worry."

But she did. Horribly. Because she was already living on borrowed time. And she still hadn't figured out a way to save Shade from himself.

As it was, she half expected Joshua to pop up at any moment with orders for her to return home. What, she wondered wretchedly, was she going to do?

Shade watched the frown move across her luscious lips, saw the shadow darken her eyes and wondered yet again how her thoughts could be so obvious one minute, then prove frustratingly unfathomable seconds later.

He would give anything to know what the hell she was thinking when she drifted away from him as she was doing now. He was going crazy trying to read the secret she held just behind her eyes.

Shade had always considered himself a good judge of character. In his line of work, a guy had to be or he wouldn't last long enough to earn his first anniversary letter from the director. Yet, as much as he hated to admit it, Rachel Parrish, or whoever she was, had him stumped.

He'd tried taking all the facts—the few he knew—about her and comparing them to what he felt about her. The problem was, nothing lined up.

Was she the secretive Mata Hari that Liz McGee kept insisting she was? Or the dedicated woman who was risking her own life to save the life of someone she loved? Was she, perhaps, that passionate, strangely vulnerable young woman who felt so right in his arms?

Or, perhaps she was all three.

Which was real? Which was an act?

He wanted to believe the best of Rachel, but he'd taken off the rose-colored glasses years ago and knew that the world was a cruel place.

Life could be petty, violent, cruel and unpredictable. In that respect, it was a lot like women, he reflected, vowing to solve the frustrating puzzle that was Rachel Parrish before this shared adventure was over.

"Oh!" An alabaster palace with tall, wedding-cake spires suddenly appeared through the silvery fog, reminding her of Brigadoon rising from the mists. "Isn't that absolutely lovely!"

"The most beautiful sight I've ever seen," he agreed.

But Shade was not looking at the palace situated on the island in the middle of the lake. He was looking down at Rachel.

She blushed. Her heart began drumming. Too fast and too hard. Her blood warmed. Too fast and too hot.

"You shouldn't talk to me that way," she protested softly.

"Afraid I'll get too close?" He ran a hand down her wind-tousled hair. He liked the fact that she'd stopped tying it back in that ugly bun. It was wet with mist; the fog droplets glistened like diamonds strewn over polished gold.

"Yes." She shook her head. "I mean, no."

He slipped his arms around her waist and felt her body begin to quiver. "Which is it?" He touched his lips to her temple. "Yes?" Her cheek. "Or no?" He nipped lightly at her lower lip, felt her sigh, then soothed the faint pain with his tongue.

"Both." She closed her eyes and leaned into the embrace, allowing herself the stolen pleasure. "It's not right, this way you make me feel."

"Not right for either one of us," Shade agreed. There was no use denying, even to himself, *especially* to himself, that she'd gotten to him. "But that doesn't change the fact that I want you."

And I want you, she could have said but didn't.

"I'm afraid of you," Rachel said instead. She felt his hands moving up and down her back and tried not to think that they felt as if they belonged there. "Of myself." She lifted her own hands to his shoulders. "Of us."

"Join the club." His hands drifted below her waist, settling on her hips, drawing her closer.

She tilted her head back and looked up at him. "Are you saying—"

"I'm afraid of us, too," he revealed, every bit as surprised to hear himself saying the words as she was to be hearing them.

"You are?"

Rachel, who thought she'd known everything about Shade, was surprised. She'd not have thought he could ever fear anything. She lifted a hand to his cheek.

"I never imagined—"

"I dream of you, dammit!" The frustration had been building for days. Shade could no longer rein it in. He grabbed hold of her slender wrist, then found, to his distraction, that he could not toss it aside. "Not just at night, but during the day.

"I think of you when I should be thinking of how I'm going to get into that damn prison. I look at the blueprints, and instead of stones and tunnels and iron bars, I see your exquisite face.

"If that isn't bad enough, I lie awake nights, thinking of your scent, your taste—like cooling rain one minute, heated honey the next—the touch of your satiny skin."

As if to underscore his words, he stroked the inside of her wrist before finally dropping her hand, but not before she'd felt his fingers tremble.

"Although it's dangerous, though I can't afford any distractions right now, I can't stop wondering what it is about you that's gotten under my skin. What secret you possess that makes you so different from any woman I've ever known. Or ever wanted. I just don't know what the hell it is."

Frustrated, angry and filled with self-disgust at showing Rachel his weakness, he dragged his hand through his hair.

The heated, obviously unplanned declaration took Rachel's breath away. Warning bells tolled. Knowing it would be one more serious infraction she would eventually have to answer for, she ignored them.

"Why do you have to know?" she asked quietly. She gave him a long, searching look. "Isn't it enough just to feel?"

"Not for me, dammit!" He took her shoulders, stopping himself short of shaking her. "You just don't get it, do you?"

Rachel refused to cower under his furious gaze. She'd faced far worse in her lifetime without succumbing to feminine vapors; she refused to flinch just because Shade was having problems dealing with the tender, generous side of his nature she'd always known he possessed. And he'd always denied.

"Get what?" she inquired calmly.

"I don't *want* to feel anything. I don't want to think of you. I don't want to worry about keeping you safe after we cross the border tomorrow morning and I damn well don't want to want you."

His fingers tightened, digging into the flesh beneath her scarlet sweater in a way she knew would leave bruises. "I don't want any part of you, Sister Rachel. I want you out of my head. Out of my life."

Her eyes possessed a hard brightness, but there was no filming of tears. She felt sorrow for the little boy who'd experienced so much pain; she felt anger for the man who stubbornly refused to see the truth.

"Caring for someone isn't such a bad thing, Shade."

"That goes to show how much you know."

Caring made you vulnerable, something Shade had vowed at a young age never to be again. His mind flashed back to his mother, who, when he was seven years old, dropped him off at the movie theater one wintry Saturday morning, promising to come back and get him.

The movie, he remembered with vivid, unrelenting clarity, had been *The Sound of Music*, about a large, loving family so far removed from his own bleak experience it could have been set on Mars.

He'd sat through every showing, watched the Roadrunner outsmart the coyote over and over again and suffered innumerable suggestions that nirvana, in the form of unaffordable popcorn, candy and Coca-Cola, was available in the lobby.

When his mother still hadn't returned by the time the theater closed for the night, Shade had gone looking for her, afraid he was going to find her sick. Or passed out. Again.

He'd diligently made the rounds of all the bars he knew she frequented. Then he'd gone back to their apartment, hoping to find her in bed with one of her boyfriends.

But instead he'd found the apartment empty. More than empty. It had been stripped. Every single thing belonging to his mother was gone. The only things that remained were his extra pair of jeans and two worn and faded New England Patriots T-shirts. The cupboards and the refrigerator, which never were all that well stocked, were empty. Even his toothbrush had disappeared.

The following morning, he'd sat on the floor, trying to figure out where he was going to get enough money to buy some food—with the exception of a package of red licorice whips, he hadn't eaten for twenty-four hours—when the landlady showed up with the social services people in tow.

He'd never seen his mother again.

Rachel watched the scowl cross his face and suspected that this was one time she knew exactly what Shade was thinking. She was afraid that she'd been overly optimistic when she vowed that before her time on earth was up, she'd teach Shade to trust.

Because, unfortunately, life had already provided its own harsh lesson. Again and again.

"I'm not asking you for anything, Shade." She touched her fingers to his cheek and felt his face harden, muscle by muscle. "Nothing at all."

That was, Shade considered grimly, part of the trouble. If she didn't ask for a future, how the hell was he going to tell her that it just wasn't in the cards? How could he give her all the reasons, sane, logical reasons, why it wouldn't work? He'd always avoided discussions about relationships, finding them a great deal like skating on the thin ice of a frozen lake. One false move and you could be trapped, over your head in the freezing water, with no way to escape.

He was saved from responding by the arrival of the boat at the dock. "We're here."

"Yes." She followed his gaze to the limousine waiting at the pier. "I wish I'd thought to brush up on my curtsy."

He ran his hand down her hair, loving the feel of the honey-hued silk against his palm. "You'll do fine."

"I hope so. I'd hate to create an international incident." Her smile touched her eyes, giving her a sweetness, a gentleness, that once again pulled an unwelcome chord inside Shade.

Temptation stirred. As he helped Rachel off the boat, Shade forced it down.

Rachel needn't have worried about royal protocol. The royal family immediately put her at ease. Upon arriving at the fairy-tale palace, she was introduced to Prince Burke, the regent of Montacroix, the man who had, before his wedding to the former Sabrina Darling last year, been declared the most eligible bachelor in the world.

The prince was the requisite tall, dark and handsome, with a lean, intelligent face and dark eyes that looked as if they never missed a thing. His American actress bride, with her striking palomino fall of pale blond hair, was equally beautiful.

Also on hand to greet their visitors were Prince Burke's father, Prince Eduard and his mother, Jessica Giraudeau. Like her daughter-in-law, Jessica had also been an acclaimed American actress. Unlike Sabrina, who continued to work at her craft, Jessica had willingly turned her back on a very successful film career for a life with the man she loved.

Standing on the other side of Prince Burke was his still-unmarried sister, the Princess Noel, a lovely, Grace Kelly type of blonde. The genuine welcome in her greeting and the warmth in her violet-blue eyes belied her cool appearance.

"And of course you know Caine," Burke said with a wave of the hand toward a tall, dark-haired man.

"Of course." Shade shook the man's hand. Rachel watched his lips curve in a seldom-used, relaxed smile. "Caine, you're looking well." His gaze moved to the woman standing beside Caine O'Bannion. "And you, princess, are as gorgeous as ever. Obviously, motherhood agrees with you."

Caine's wife, the Princess Chantal, who'd once kept an entire army of tabloid paparazzi working overtime to keep up with her jet-set life-style, laughingly greeted Shade with a hug and a kiss—continental style—on both cheeks.

Although still glamorous, with her gypsy-dark hair and eyes and diamonds flashing at her ears, today she appeared every bit the young matron. A toddler clung to her red silk trousers.

When introduced to Rachel, Chantal's eyes slid from Rachel to Shade, then back to Rachel. In them Rachel could see the same womanly sympathy she'd viewed in Marianne's knowing gaze.

Shade had met Chantal's husband, a former presidential security guard, when their paths had crossed during a presidential trip to Athens. During their transatlantic flight, Shade had told Rachel that Caine had earned a medal for throwing himself in front of the president, subsequently taking a bullet from a would-be assassin's gun.

Caine had met Chantal when he'd been assigned to provide protection for her during an American tour to raise funds for the Rescue the Children Fund three years ago. Weeks after saving her life, he'd opened up a Washington, D.C., security business with his partner, then gone to Montacroix to propose to the headstrong princess.

Chantal had not been the only member of the royal family whose life had been in peril. Caine told Rachel about an assassination attempt against Burke. Fortunately, the prince had escaped with minor injuries, although sadly, a woman casino employee involved in the plot had been killed to ensure her silence.

They spent the night at the palace, where, over a superb dinner, Rachel charmed Eduard by displaying a surprising familiarity with Montacroix's past.

"I'm amazed you know so much about our country," Burke said, his admiration obvious.

Rachel smiled, ignoring Shade's sharp glance. "I've always enjoyed history."

Later that night, even though the canopied antique bed—which had once belonged to the Empress Josephine, Chantal revealed—was extremely comfortable, fit for a princess, Rachel couldn't sleep.

Slipping into an ivory silk robe, she opened the French doors leading out onto the balcony and discovered that she was not the only one finding sleep a difficult target.

Only a few feet away, Shade, who'd left his room next door, was leaning with his forearms against the stone balustrade, gazing out over the moon-gilded lake.

Rachel felt a sudden urge to go to him, to wrap her arms around his waist, to press her body tight against his back, to hold on and never let go.

She slipped her hands into the pockets of her robe to stop herself from giving in to her unruly impulses. But she could not resist joining Shade on the balcony.

He turned as she approached, and Rachel was surprised to see that he was smoking. "I'm sorry," she said quietly. "I didn't mean to disturb you."

"You always disturb me." His expression, in the slanting moonlight, was not the least bit welcoming.

"If you'd like, I'll go back indoors."

"I'd like you to go back to Washington. Or Salem, or wherever the hell you're really from. But, since you've already insisted on continuing on to Yaznovia, you might as well stay."

It was certainly not the most gracious invitation she'd ever received. But unwilling to part with his company, and knowing that he had a great deal on his mind, Rachel decided not to waste precious time sulking.

"It's a lovely night," she murmured. The sky was clear, the night cool. "You can't see nearly that many stars in the city. And the moonlight makes the lake look like polished silver."

He didn't answer. Instead, he turned away again and looked out over the palace grounds. Rachel watched the brief red glow as he drew in on the cigarette.

"When did you start smoking again?" He'd quit, she knew, during his torturous time in the general's prison.

"Tonight. It was either smoking or sex." He took another long drag and wished he hadn't. The burning tobacco tasted awful. He couldn't remember why he'd ever enjoyed it.

"You know, of course, that smoking isn't good for you."

"I've never believed in denying my baser cravings." He turned toward her again, his eyes hard, his mouth curved in a grim slash of a humorless smile. "Want to help me with the other?"

She felt the embarrassing rise of heat in her face and blessed the darkness. "If you're trying to scare me away, Shade, it isn't going to work."

He stood there for a long, silent time, just looking at her. Refusing to back down, Rachel matched his unblinking gaze with a level look of her own.

Shade had never met anyone like Rachel Parrish. His inability to intimidate the woman both amazed and irritated him. Most women—hell, most people—foolish enough to try to face down his cold, silent stare immediately crumpled. But not Rachel. She was as tough inside as she was soft outside.

Her earlier words ran a belated warning bell. "How did you know I used to smoke?"

It was Rachel's turn to shrug. She'd made another tactical error. "It was merely an educated guess."

"An educated guess." Shade didn't even try to hide his disbelief. "You're driving me up a wall, Sister Rachel."

"I'm sorry."

"Sorry enough to tell me where we've met?"

When she didn't answer, he cursed, not a gentlemanly oath, but a rude, savage word that made her blush burn hotter.

"Get to bed, Rachel." He dropped the unwanted cigarette to the stone underfoot and ground it beneath the heel of his boot. "We've got a long day tomorrow."

He turned away. She looked at his rigid back, wishing against hope that there was something, anything, she could do to make things better. Some half-truth she could tell him to ease his distrust. But the sad fact was that without admitting the absolute truth, which he undoubtedly wouldn't believe, either, there was nothing she could say or do that would change things.

Blinking back her tears, she wrapped her robe more tightly around her and returned to her bedroom.

The last thing she heard, before she closed the French doors, was a savage curse and the sound of a match striking.

The next morning, after a long and sleepless night, Shade and Rachel prepared for the final and most dangerous part of their long journey.

Caine and Burke accompanied them out to the garage, where they retrieved the armored Mercedes sedan the prince had arranged to have waiting for them. The car had been bullet proofed by an Italian firm specializing in such customizing demanded by European industrialists and Saudi sheikhs; the engine was strong enough to outrun any trouble they might encounter along the way.

Knowing that food was scarce in Yaznovia, Burke had given them a large basket filled with gourmet items from the royal kitchens.

"If there's anything I can do," Caine said, shaking hands with Shade, "anything at all, just let me know. Chantal and I will be staying here for the next two weeks."

"You're a family man now, O'Bannion," Shade reminded the other man unnecessarily. "With different responsibilities."

"Still—"

"If I get in a bind, I'll call." Shade glanced over at Rachel, who'd been even more quiet than usual. "Or Rachel will."

The fact that Rachel would only telephone in the event that Shade could not was readily apparent to all four individuals in the garage.

"Be careful." Caine's expression was grave. As was Prince Burke's.

Shade's grin was at odds with the seriousness of the situation. "Piece of cake."

8

BOTH RACHEL AND SHADE were silent as they left the palace, driving past the formal gardens and velvet lawn, then finally, back through the elaborately stylized wrought-iron gates.

The narrow road to the border twisted like a corkscrew through the woods. Dark green pine trees scented the air. Snowcapped Alpine mountains rose in the distance; their destination was on the other side of those white-capped peaks.

"You're awfully quiet this morning," Shade observed.

"I was just thinking."

"I was afraid of that." His tone was one of gentle teasing, devoid of its usual sarcastic edge. "I don't suppose you'd care to share your thoughts with me."

Rachel wondered what Shade would say if he knew that she'd come to the reluctant decision, sometime during the long sleepless night, that if Shade pushed the issue, if he insisted on making love to her, she would not tell him no.

She was all too aware that a sin of such magnitude would carry with it an enormous cost. But she refused to dwell on that right now. Because, during the predawn hours, she'd come to the conclusion that to experience such bliss, such love, in Shade's strong arms would be worth any price she might later have to pay.

She sucked in a deep breath, then let it out on a slow, soft sigh. When she hesitated, Shade experienced the now-familiar urge to shake her. Of all the weapons Rachel Parrish had at her command—and he'd discovered to both his surprise and his chagrin that she had several—evasion was her most well honed.

He shook his head with self disgust. He could not believe how dangerously close he was coming to being crazy about a woman he didn't dare trust.

As if sensing his frustration, Rachel placed her hand on his leg. "Actually," she said, not quite truthfully, "I was thinking about your plan to kill the general."

He covered her hand with his free left one, linking their fingers loosely together. "Don't."

She couldn't allow the steely warning in his tone to deter her from her mission. "Have you considered what it will feel like, having to go through the rest of your life with another man's murder on your conscience?"

"Tell you what—why don't you worry about your own conscience, Sister Rachel? Because mine is just fine, thank you."

"But—"

Shade cut her off with a curse. He shook his head in mute disgust. "Traveling with you is like taking a trip with Jiminy Cricket."

The unfamiliar reference flew over her head and his eyes were unreadable behind the dark smoke-gray lenses of his aviator sunglasses. But Rachel got Shade's meaning. Loud and clear.

"You can't do it," she insisted.

"Now that's where you're dead wrong, sweetheart," he returned grimly. "I can do it. And I will."

Frustrated to a point near tears, Rachel wondered what it was going to take to get through to him. She refused to consider the possibility that she might fail. The idea was too horrific to contemplate. As they drove toward their destination, through the thick forest, past rushing rivers, Shade found himself once again unwillingly intrigued. How was it that a woman who harbored so many damn secrets could also be an unwavering bastion of morality?

She was definitely a woman of contrasts. And the more time he spent in her company, the more Shade determined that before this little escapade was over, he would have discovered everything there was to know about the lady.

He maneuvered the armored Mercedes through a series of hairpin switchbacks. Rachel watched and admired the casual, confident way his hands loosely held the walnut steering wheel, delicately guiding the car through the tight turns.

As they came out of the final curve, they both saw it: a concrete bunker with gun slits perched atop a limestone promontory above the road.

"The border," Rachel breathed. Her heart was pounding hard and fast in her chest. Her blood rang in her ears like a tom-tom.

"Show time," Shade agreed as he began to brake. A hundred yards away was a small white building.

She watched as he underwent a metamorphosis that was as fascinating as it was unsettling. Although there was nothing the slightest bit malleable about Shade, during these past days together, she'd witnessed his compassion and caught fleeting glimpses of tenderness. And despite the seriousness of their mission, she'd even seen him relax.

But now, as they approached the wooden barricade manned by a pair of uniformed soldiers, he appeared to come to attention. Every muscle in his body went rigid—his back, his arms, his neck, his jaw, even that intriguing muscle defined by the scar carving its jagged way up his cheek. Although she still couldn't see his eyes, she knew that behind the dark lenses, they would be emerald hard.

"Let me do the talking."

"I wouldn't have it any other way." Her shaky voice betrayed her discomfort with the situation.

As he downshifted, he slanted her an unreadable sideways glance. "There's still time to change your mind."

She stiffened her own back, both literally and figuratively. "I'm not going to change my mind."

He chuckled, but the sound held scant humor. "I can't decide whether you're the craziest woman I've ever met, or simply the most stubborn. But either way, I'll give you this, Sister Rachel. You've got guts."

They'd reached the barricade. Surprising her yet again, Shade reached out and gave her knee a quick, reassuring squeeze. "It's going to be all right."

Rachel prayed he was right.

A soldier, clad in a brown uniform with red trim, exited the guardhouse. One look at the Sam Browne belt slung across his broad chest made Rachel's mouth go dry. It was one thing to witness vicariously the danger that was part and parcel of Shade's life. To experience it firsthand was numbing.

The guard had a deadly looking 9 mm pistol pointed directly at them. An assault rifle Shade recognized to be a Yaznovian variation of the Soviet Kalashnikov was slung over his shoulder.

Shade took off the sunglasses and rolled down the car window. "Good afternoon."

Rachel, silent beside Shade, folded her hands tightly together in her lap and admired his ability to feign such an easy tone.

The man did not return the smile. He gestured with the automatic pistol and demanded their papers. Rachel pulled hers from her bag with nerveless fingers and handed them to Shade, who in turn gave them to the guard.

She held her breath as he studied her forged documents, his dark eyes moving from her photograph to her face. Apparently satisfied, he turned his attention to Shade's documents, this time studying them in more detail. As the seconds dragged on, Rachel's nerves began to scream.

"You are in the armaments business?" He spoke in a rough, heavily accented English.

"I sell weapons," Shade agreed. "The newest and the best western technology has to offer. I've come to Yaznovia to meet with the general. You should have been notified." His frown portrayed his irritation at this petty bureaucratic procedure.

"We received a dispatch from the war ministry this morning. About you." The man's gaze returned to Rachel. "And your traveling companion."

"Ms. Parrish is my administrative assistant."

"That's what the dispatch said." The guard grinned for the first time since they'd arrived at the border. The wicked slash suggested he'd already drawn his own conclusions regarding Rachel's business qualifications and her relationship to Shade.

The wolfish grin faded. "You must both get out of the car." As if to reinforce the command, he reached down and yanked the door handle open.

Shade felt Rachel tense beside him and damned himself for allowing her to come along. This mission was risky enough without having to worry about keeping her out of the clutches of the general's goons. He'd never forgive himself if she ended up being raped. Or worse, killed.

"Is there a problem with the papers?"

"You will not ask questions. You will both come with me. Now."

Biting back a curse, Shade stepped out onto the road. Rachel climbed out of the car on legs that were not nearly as steady as she would have liked.

"Whatever happens," Shade murmured in a low voice, for her ears only, "do exactly what I say. Without asking any questions. And don't panic."

"I had no intention of panicking."

Assuring Shade of that important fact served to calm herself. By the time they reached the guardhouse, Rachel's heart had returned to its normal beat and her hands, while still cold, were no longer blocks of ice.

"You will come inside. While I telephone the ministry." The guard gestured with his pistol, leaving them no choice.

Shade cupped his fingers around Rachel's elbow. Together they entered a frame structure that was even smaller than it appeared from the outside. There was barely enough room for the four of them.

The other guard, whose single red chevron on his sleeve revealed him to be outranked by the first, jumped to attention the minute they entered the guardhouse. The magazine he'd been perusing fell to the floor.

Rachel took one glance at the buxom brunette Penthouse pet-of-the-month, and felt the hot color flood into her cheeks.

"You've definitely got Miss April beat," Shade murmured. "In spades."

Her color deepened, from embarrassment and forbidden pleasure that Shade found her desirable.

The soldier seemed to agree. While the first placed the call to the war ministry, the younger guard lounged against the wall, his arms folded across the front of his chest, and gave Rachel a slow but thorough perusal.

As his pale blue eyes crawled over her face, lingering for a horribly long time on her breasts before continuing their journey down her legs, clad in a pair of skin-tight red leather jeans, Rachel wondered how it was that when Shade looked at her in much the same way, her body warmed, her heart pounded and her bones felt on the verge of melting. This man's gaze made her feel as if a thousand spiders were crawling over her flesh.

Shade was trying to listen to the phone conversation. From the man's frown, as he studied a map on his desk, Shade suspected there might be some problem developing.

He knew it was vital that he be prepared to act quickly. But his attention was diverted by the way the guard's beady little eyes were pawing their way over Rachel.

Something hot and dangerous stirred within Shade. Something that felt uncomfortably like jealousy.

Whatever it was, Shade had a sudden urge to put his fist down the jerk's throat. And to give him a swift hard kick where it would hurt the most and leave him unable to even consider having sex with any woman for a very long time.

One hand curled into an unconscious fist at his side. With the other he pulled Rachel against him. Hard.

"She's taken." His voice was as clear and as dangerous as shards of broken glass.

There was a brief standoff as the men's gazes locked. Rachel's disgust and fear disintegrated, replaced instead by a very strong female pique. The two of them were behaving like a pair of stags in rutting season, butting heads over a female prize.

She was about to complain, when the voice of the older guard, speaking on the telephone, reminded her of the danger of this situation. Her identity was that of Shade's lover. If she refused to play her part, she could end up getting Shade killed.

She wasn't concerned for herself. After Salem, what more could happen to her?

Pushing down her irritation, she turned toward him and put her hand on his chest. "Darling, is this going to take very much longer?" Her voice was soft and breathy, designed to make a man think of sin and sex. "You promised me we'd be at that nice, romantic Alpine inn by now." There was not the slightest doubt as to what they'd do once they arrived at the hotel.

Pleased at how fast she'd picked up on his ploy, Shade ran the back of his hand down her cheek. "Soon," he promised.

"I certainly hope so." She breathed a deep sigh, causing her breasts to rise and fall beneath the snug red sweater. "I hate waiting." A thought occurred to Rachel. A wonderful, clever idea she knew Shade would find absolutely brilliant. "Especially when you promised I'd meet the general."

As she'd hoped, her pronouncement garnered the immediate attention of the two guards. "I do so hope he likes me." On instinct, she bit her bottom lip, catching the crimson-tinted flesh seductively between her straight white teeth.

Shade had to quash another sudden impulse to wring Rachel's lissome neck. It was one thing to pretend that she was his lover. Quite another to suggest that she might be destined for the general's bed.

"How could he not?" Shade muttered, having no choice but to play along. For now.

Her words appeared to have the desired effect upon her audience. The guard turned away, but Shade could hear the rapid, one-sided telephone conversation. A moment later the man put down the phone and turned back to them.

"The minister will meet you in Karikistan." He took a red felt pen and circled a small town on the map. "In two days. From there you will be escorted by armed guard to the general's compound."

The village in question was approximately twenty-five kilometers away. Which wouldn't be any problem, in any other country. But there was one thing everyone appeared to have overlooked.

"How are we supposed to get through the capital?" The city had been under siege from snipers for months.

The guard shrugged dismissively as he returned their papers. "That is your problem."

As they returned to the Mercedes and drove through the raised red-and-white barricade, Rachel wondered what was wrong with Shade. He was seething with barely restrained fury. It had to be more than the fact that they were not to be given a proper military escort through the war zone. After all, Shade had warned her from the start that they'd probably be on their own. He hadn't expected any assistance from the general's forces.

No, whatever he was upset about—and he was more furious than she'd ever seen him—seemed to have something to do with her.

"Are you angry at me?" she asked after being submitted to his stony silence for ten minutes. Minutes that seemed like hours.

He didn't take his eyes from the winding road. "Angry doesn't begin to cover it."

"What did I do wrong? You told me not to panic. I didn't panic. I didn't slap that horrid guard for undressing me with his lecherous eyes and I pretended, as well as I could, to be your mistress. I believe I did everything you told me to do."

"I told you to let me do the talking." His fingers tightened to a death grip on the steering wheel. "Christ, lady, you let those goons, not to mention everyone at the war ministry, think I was pimping for the damn general."

She stared at him blankly. "Is that all you're concerned about? Your reputation?"

"*My* reputation?" He shot her a brief, incredulous look. "How about yours?"

"My cover, which you selected without bothering to discuss with me, is to play the role of your lover," Rachel reminded him mildly. "What's so different about implying that the general might also be interested in my favors?"

He slammed on the brakes; Rachel had to reach out and put her hand on the dashboard to keep from being flung into the windshield.

"Because what you and I have is different!" Shade exploded.

The words were out before he could censor them. Hell, Shade considered grimly, that's what he got for letting his damn mouth override his normally cautious brain.

Rachel smiled, despite the fact that they were driving into untold dangers, despite the gravity of their situation, despite all the reasons why an intimate relationship with Shade was unwise, pleasure shimmered through her.

He loved her, whether he wanted to admit it or not. Just as she loved him.

"Yes." Her gray eyes were very clear and very certain. "It is very different."

It came to him suddenly, unexpected and unwanted, like a sucker punch to the gut. He could care about this woman. He could love her. The idea was more terrifying than an entire nation of armed criminals.

They sat there, looking at each other in the afternoon Alpine light. Silence stretched between them, speaking more eloquently than words.

Just when Rachel thought Shade was going to say something significant, he shook his head, grimaced and announced, "We'd better get going. These mountains are overrun with snipers and it's a helluva lot harder to hit a moving target."

Which, Shade considered with grim humor, was precisely the strategy he'd always used to avoid romantic entanglements. Until now. Until Rachel.

They continued down the winding mountainside. Caught up in their own thoughts, neither spoke.

TO CALL THE CAPITAL CITY a war zone was a vast understatement. The sound of mortars boomed over piles of stone that had once been comfortable homes. High-rise offices had been reduced to rubble. Instead of the industrious sound of car horns on the city streets, the sharp retort of rifle fire, as snipers shot randomly from atop roofs of whatever buildings remained standing, rang through the air.

The sidewalks, stained a muddy reddish brown with blood from fallen citizens, resembled sprint tracks. Yaznovians, when forced outside the relative safety of their homes in search of food, water or cooking fuel, ran everywhere, staying, when possible, close to walls, pausing behind trees and parked cars, dashing across open streets, literally running for their lives.

Street signs, riddled with bullet holes, were unreadable. Stone statues, erected in honor of past leaders, had been defaced or torn down.

A city park, where once families had picnicked beneath leafy chestnut trees, had been turned into a graveyard. Rows of fresh earthen mounds had risen where children should have played.

Rachel felt as if she were looking straight into the fires of hell.

She knew she should be terrified. And she was. But she also had complete faith in Shade's survival instincts. Instincts he'd honed well over the years.

He drove the Mercedes through the side streets, avoiding fleeing pedestrians with a deft skill that Rachel admired. A shot hit the rear passenger window and was deflected by the bullet-proof glass. Rachel jumped and turned white. Her blood froze. But she did not scream.

The woman definitely had spunk, Shade considered. She was tough in ways that were at direct odds with her seemingly innocent vulnerability. It was no wonder he was falling in love with her. No wonder she had him thinking of a future even though he knew such thoughts were impossible.

"We're almost there," he assured her. "Just keep that gorgeous head down."

The compliment, offered so casually, almost managed to expunge her fear. Almost. But not quite. Rachel wrapped her arms around her knees, lowered her head and squeezed her eyes tightly closed. And then she prayed.

Shade suddenly pulled the car into a courtyard that was surrounded on three sides by high stone walls. "End of the road," he announced, not bothering to hide his own relief that the hair-raising race through the city streets was finally over. At least for now.

Rachel risked a glance out the window. "A tavern?" Although the wine the other night had made her head spin, at this moment she would not have refused a calming drink.

"It's owned by a friend of mine."

"What if he isn't here?" She was trying to be brave, but the idea of going back out into that shooting gallery was decidedly unpalatable.

"He isn't. Jake escaped to Montacroix, then on to Switzerland last month," Shade revealed. "But I have a key. And there's an apartment above the bar where we can spend the night."

A vision shimmered through her mind. A warm, seductive picture of a cozy room, a thick feather bed, and Shade. The idea of spending the night in his arms was every bit as enticing as it was forbidden.

As Shade watched her wide eyes cloud, their thoughts tangled. He was drawn to her in ways he couldn't remember ever being drawn to any other woman.

His hand slipped beneath her silken hair. His fingers brushed the nape of her neck with a gentle touch.

He leaned toward her slowly, allowing her time to read his intention and back away.

But she didn't. Instead, every bit as seduced as he, Rachel moistened her lips and waited.

Their mouths were a whisper apart. She placed her fingertips against his khaki shirt and felt his heart thudding in a strong, sure rhythm that matched the beat of her own.

Closer. Then closer still. She could feel the warmth of his breath.

And then, just as his lips brushed hers, a scream shattered the suspended silence.

"What the hell?" Shade jerked his head back and looked around, his body as tense as it had been earlier at the border crossing.

A child, a boy, no more than eight or nine years old, came dashing out of the door of the neighboring building and began pounding on the car window.

"It's my mother," he shouted in obvious panic. "You must help her! She's dying!"

9

THE BOY'S MOTHER WASN'T dying, Rachel determined after they entered an apartment barren of furniture. In the center of the room, lying on a tablecloth on the bare floor was a woman, obviously pregnant and drenched in sweat.

Rachel knelt down and began to examine the woman, who, unlike her son, spoke no English. She didn't need to. The agony and fear etched into every line of her face needed no translation. The entire time her hands moved over the swollen, undulating belly, Rachel talked in low, soothing tones.

And then she smiled, patted the woman's cheek and turned back to the nervously waiting boy.

"Your mother will be fine," she assured him. "She's simply going to have a baby."

"Now?" Shade looked nearly as panic-stricken as the boy.

"Tonight," Rachel determined.

"Can't she wait?"

"I suppose she might." Rachel rolled up her sleeves and went over to the kitchen area—little more than a sink, refrigerator and wood-burning stove against the far wall—to wash her hands. The small stack of oak and pine piled up beside the stove revealed what had happened to the furniture. "But the baby won't."

Shade swore.

Rachel turned on the tap. "At least there's hot water."

"The entire block is built on hot springs."

"Lucky." She rubbed a bar of brown soap between her hands, rinsed them and, lacking any sterile toweling, shook them dry.

"That's not exactly the word I'd use." He shot a look at the woman writhing on the floor across the room. "Hell."

"Why don't you stop cursing and make yourself useful?" Rachel asked with a calm Shade found amazing, considering the circumstances.

"Doing what?"

"Boiling some water would be a good start."

"I thought they only did that in movies."

"It's important to sterilize the knife," Rachel explained calmly over the woman's piercing scream. "And we'll need some clean towels."

For the first time since her arrival on earth, she felt inordinately self-assured. Fortunately, childbirth was one thing that hadn't changed all that much in three hundred years. Oh, admittedly some of the techniques and equipment might have become more modern, but human biology was the same as it had been in the 1600s.

"A knife? You're not going to try to perform a cesarean?" Shade wasn't up on the medical qualifications of midwives, but he knew damn well that surgery wasn't high on the list.

The woman screeched again and began cursing like a Yaznovian lumberjack. Her tortured voice reminded him of the screams that had echoed through the stone walls of the general's prison during the interminable torture sessions. Amazingly, Shade considered, Rachel seemed unmoved by the sound.

"The knife is to cut the cord." Another bloodcurdling scream that went on and on ricocheted around the apartment. "I'd better get to work." She nodded toward the stove. "And so should you."

"Gee, Miz Rachel," he drawled, "I don't know nothin' 'bout birthin' no babies."

His uneasy attempt at humor was wasted on Rachel, who'd never seen Butterfly McQueen deliver her famous movie line. "You will before the night's over," she promised.

The labor, blessedly, proved relatively uneventful. Rachel was grateful that, although the woman was undernourished, she was young and strong. Her husband, they learned, had gone out that morning in search of food for his family and had not returned.

Afternoon turned to evening. Then night. Tracers lit the darkened sky, creating a strobelike effect in the little room.

Since it was too dangerous to send the boy away, Rachel put him to work, soothing his mother's sweaty brow with cool cloths dampened with locally grown lavender oil. She had Shade translate her instructions regarding the importance of relaxation and proper breathing during labor—the once-radical technique that had gotten her into such trouble three hundred years ago—and then she taught him how to coach the woman through each contraction. And how to massage the undulating belly. Although awkward and endearingly self-conscious at first, he soon caught on. As Shade relaxed, the woman did, as well, which eased her discomfort considerably.

The beautifully simple technique declared heresy in her day, only to evolve into the much-lauded Lamaze method centuries later, was a vast improvement over tying the woman's wrists to the bedpost and shoving a birthing stick between her teeth, Rachel considered.

The four strangers began to mesh, to work smoothly together as a team: Rachel, Shade, the woman and her son, all united in a single purpose.

Five hours after the boy's desperate plea for help, the woman gave one final push and the baby eased slickly out of its mother's womb into Rachel's waiting hands.

Everyone in the room held their collective breaths, waiting for the infant's cry. A cry that began as a weak, stuttering whimper and quickly escalated into a full, healthy wail.

"You have a daughter," Rachel said, smiling through her happy tears as she placed the baby girl on the woman's stomach and cut the cord that had bonded child and mother for nine months.

She did not need Shade to translate. The new mother, overcome by such joy in the midst of the horror raging outdoors, began to cry and kissed Rachel's hands. Then Shade's. Then she hugged her son and cried all the harder.

Capping off the blessed event, the absent husband chose that moment to burst through the door. He had managed to locate some precious loaves of brown bread and goat cheese and, miraculously, two bottles of wine. Viewing his triumphant wife and newborn daughter, he dropped his bundles to the floor.

There was more laughter. More happy tears. Even Shade's eyes, Rachel noticed, were suspiciously wet. Glasses were raised as toasts were made to the baby.

The new mother. The baby's older brother. To Shade. And, of course, there were several toasts to Rachel, who, the husband insisted, was an angel.

Finally, taking the blessings of the Yaznovian family with them, Shade and Rachel slipped out of the building, retrieved their luggage and food from the Mercedes and made their way through the tavern to the upstairs apartment.

Shade closed the shutters and risked lighting a candle. The apartment, like the one next door, consisted of a single room with a kitchen area against one wall and an adjoining bath. A large hand-carved bed, covered with a thick feather comforter, dominated the small space.

Shade put the suitcases on the floor and the picnic basket on the table. "You must be exhausted."

She was tired. Strange how she hadn't noticed it earlier. But of course her mind had been on other things. She rubbed the back of her neck.

"Not as exhausted as the baby's mother." She smiled with reminiscent pleasure. "Wasn't that wonderful?"

"You were wonderful." He wrapped his arms around her, lowered his head and pressed his lips to hers. "I think this is where I tell you I'm very impressed."

Her lips curved beneath his. "I was just doing my job."

"I know. It's just that I..."

When his voice trailed off, she tilted her head back and met his oddly embarrassed gaze with a fond one of her own. "You didn't believe I really was a midwife."

"I guess I didn't. Not really." He ran his palm down her hair. "The idea just seemed so—"

"Old-fashioned?"

"Yeah." Shade decided not to ruin the moment by pointing out that she hadn't exactly been a model of veracity during their time together.

His wide hand continued down her back, creating warmth. And desire. Rachel loved him so much, she wanted him so much, she twined her arms around his neck. "I guess I'm just an old-fashioned woman." She wanted to melt into him.

Shade wanted her to do exactly that. "My favorite kind."

He kissed her. Deep and hard. On and on. His hand cupped her buttocks, lifting her against his swelling groin.

A fiery knot of frustration was growing inside her. Rachel wanted to feel Shade's hot naked flesh against hers. She felt as if she would die if he didn't undress her. If he didn't take her. Now.

Her breasts pressed against his chest. Her body moved urgently against his. Shade could feel the need radiating from her. Or was it his own need he was feeling?

Shade wanted her with a hunger like nothing he'd ever known. And if she'd been any other woman, he would have already satisfied that need.

But there was something about Rachel, something innocent and unsullied, that had kept him from indulging in what he suspected would be an extraordinary sexual experience.

Every instinct Shade possessed told him that, despite the fact he still hadn't unearthed a single piece of biographical information on his mysterious companion, Rachel wasn't any danger to his life.

But she did represent other dangers that were far more deadly.

So why the hell didn't he back away? He wasn't chained to the woman. Or was he?

He broke the heated kiss off long enough to look down into her face. Her soft, flushed, exquisite face.

"If I ask you a question, one question, will you promise to tell me the absolute truth?"

At this moment, Rachel could have refused Shade nothing. "I promise."

"You have done this before, haven't you?"

He could have groaned as he viewed the telltale color rise in her cheeks. "Not exactly."

Shade was afraid he knew precisely where this was going. "Dammit, Rachel—"

"I'm sorry." She bit her lip and looked up at him with wide, vulnerable eyes. "I promised you the absolute truth, didn't I? Well." She took a deep breath. "It's true I haven't had much sexual experience." Another long pause. "Actually," she admitted reluctantly, "I haven't had any actual experience."

Hell, he'd been afraid of that all along. Although it was damn unusual to run across a virgin in this day and age, Shade reminded himself with grim humor that he'd always prided himself on managing the impossible.

Outside the window, the tracers continued to light up the sky; mortars from the distant hillside boomed like Fourth of July fireworks. Inside there was only thick, expectant silence.

"You know I want you." He ran his hands up and down her arms.

His flat tone, the regret she viewed in his eyes made Rachel's heart clench. She'd known all along Shade possessed a deep-seated trait of integrity, but why did he finally have to realize it himself at this moment?

"As I want you." She'd never, in the over three hundred years of her existence, uttered a more truthful statement.

Shade couldn't believe it. Here he was, alone with a beautiful woman with danger as an additional aphrodisiac. And if that wasn't enough, this very same woman, this sexy, beautiful, sweet woman who felt like heaven in his arms, was almost begging him to make love to her.

And what happened? A conscience he'd spent a lifetime denying suddenly decided to kick in.

"Hell, I've never claimed to be Prince Charming," he said. "But even I'm not so jaded that I have to get my sexual kicks seducing innocents."

"Are you saying that you refuse to make love with me because I'm a virgin?"

"No. I'm saying that I refuse to make love to you because, for once in my life, I'm trying to do the right thing."

"But that doesn't make any sense. If you want me, and I want you—"

"It's not about want, dammit!" He released her but didn't move away. Instead he stood over her, his dark face tense, his expression as frustrated as she'd ever seen it. "Want is easy. Too easy."

He thought about all the hours he'd wasted in bed with women who'd never succeeded in touching his heart. Just as he hadn't touched theirs.

To her added discomfort, Rachel was discovering a very mortal pride. "Perhaps it's easy for you." She tilted her chin and refused to cry. "But not for me."

His gaze softened. "No." He sighed as he cupped her face in his hand. "Not for you."

When he found himself wanting to kiss away her unhappiness, he dropped his hand again. "Which is exactly what I'm trying to say. It would never work, Rachel. You know that. And I know it."

Her head told her he was right, that a future together was utterly impossible. Her heart refused to listen.

"You're so certain of that?"

"As certain as I've ever been of anything." He shoved his hands into his jeans pockets to keep from touching her. To keep from dragging her down onto that bed and stripping that sexy mistress sweater and leather jeans from her body and burying himself in her tight, welcoming warmth. "Women like you just aren't made for short-term romantic interludes."

Once again pride rose to steamroller over her pain. She lifted a challenging brow. "Women like me?" How dare he think he could pigeonhole her so easily!

Rachel found herself almost telling Shade everything, just to watch his face when he realized exactly how much she knew about him. And how little he truly knew about her.

"You're a soft, compassionate, innocent woman. And you deserve more."

"Such as?"

Caught up in his explanation, Shade missed the warning edge to her quiet tone. "How about a husband with a boring, regular nine-to-five job that can't get him killed at any time, for starters?

"And a sprawling ranch-style house in the suburbs, and a couple of well-behaved, cute kids who'll sell Girl

Scout cookies and play Little League and make you and their dad proud."

"That doesn't sound like such a bad scenario," she admitted reluctantly. It sounded wonderful. Better than wonderful. It sounded, she reflected, like heaven on earth.

"It isn't. For some people."

"But not you."

"No." He ran a desperate hand through his hair. "Not me."

Even if he wanted to, which he didn't, Shade could not give Rachel any part of that life. His work took him all over the world, his life was constantly in peril.

Knowing nothing about parenting—having never had anything resembling a role model—he'd decided long ago not to have kids.

As for marriage, he suspected it was okay for romantic, warmhearted guys like Conlan. But not for him.

His entire life had been a hit-and-run series of adventures. Liking it that way, Shade had always narrowed his sexual relationships to women who shared his dislike of long-term commitments.

So, the smartest thing, the kindest thing, would be not to start anything with the lovely, delectable Rachel. The tension in the room was so thick Shade couldn't think straight. "I'm going out."

Alarm sprinted up her spine. "What? Why?"

"I have things to do." Like run away from this emotional quicksand.

"It's too dangerous."

Shade wondered what Rachel would say if he told her that she represented far more danger than anything he'd run into out on those deadly, mean streets. "Don't worry about me."

"I do." Another unvarnished truth.

"Don't." Unable to resist, he cupped her chin in his fingers and kissed her. A brief hot flare that ended too soon for either of them. And then he was gone.

She listened to the sound of his boots on the stairway, heard the door to the tavern squeak open. Then close.

Then, and only then, did she allow herself to weep.

She didn't know how long she'd been lying on the bed, crying her heart out into the soft down pillow. But when she heard the apartment door open, she jumped up, unable to hide her relief.

"Oh." Her welcoming smile faded as she viewed the man standing in the doorway. "Hello, Joshua."

"That's not exactly the warmest greeting I've ever received," he complained.

"I'm sorry." She sat back down on the edge of the mattress and knit her fingers together in her lap. "It's been a very trying day."

"So I saw. Congratulations on the child, by the way. You did a very exemplary job of bringing her into the world."

"Her mother did all the work."

"You were an immense help. Not to mention providing much-needed emotional comfort. And Shade wasn't half-bad, himself."

"He was pretty special, wasn't he?" Her soft voice revealed her pride. And her love.

"I had not realized the man was capable of such compassion."

"Shade is capable of a lot more than even he knows," Rachel said loyally.

"So you've always said." The older man paused, as if weighing his words, then made his decision. So what if it was against policy? he considered. It would be worth a slap on the wrist to bring that smile back to her lips.

"Would it make you feel better to know that the child you delivered tonight will grow up to be one of Yaznovia's most beloved legislators?"

"Yaznovia doesn't have a legislature," Rachel said as another burst of machine-gun fire echoed outside the window. Where was Shade? Why hadn't he returned? "It's a military dictatorship."

"For the time being. But democracy will eventually prevail. And that little girl will play a very large role in her country's future."

"Well, that's nice to hear." Her shoulders were slumped, her eyes devoid of their usual bright light. Something occurred to her. "You're not supposed to reveal the future, are you?" It was one of the first rules she'd learned that long-ago day.

"No. But I thought it might ease your distress."

"That was very nice of you. But you shouldn't have risked disciplinary action for me."

"I wanted to help." Sighing, he sat down beside her. "He'll return safely, if that's what you're worried about."

That knowledge, at least, provided some relief. "Thank you." This time she managed a frail smile that only wobbled slightly.

"I'm worried about you." He took her cold hand in his, lacing their fingers together. "And I'm not the only one. Everyone is deeply concerned about your inappropriate feelings for Shade."

"Since when is love inappropriate?"

"When it has you wishing for a life that cannot be," he said gently. Firmly. "I was sent here to bring you that warning. And your new deadline."

She closed her eyes, afraid of what she might hear. Perhaps she'd already be gone when Shade returned. She wondered if he'd miss her. If he'd think of her on lonely nights when he couldn't sleep. Or dream of her when he did.

"When?" she asked on a ragged whisper.

"You have been granted an additional seventy-two hours to save Shade Blackstone's soul."

"So soon." She felt the cold flow over her. She was numb with it. "And if that's not enough time?" Rachel knew the answer.

"If you cannot succeed by then, you will have to accept your failure, Rachel. And know that you did your best." His tone was final. He patted her hand with paternalistic fondness. "Goodbye, little one."

She watched as he faded away, like a memory disappearing into the misty past.

Deciding that she'd wallowed in self-pity long enough, Rachel took a long hot bath and willed herself to relax. Then she delved into the contents of the rattan basket, uncovering a wealth of gourmet items along with a bottle of vintage cabernet. The palace cook had also included dishes and cutlery.

She set the table and poured the wine. Then she waited for Shade to return. All the time, she was vividly aware of their valuable time ticking away.

Then, finally, she heard his footfalls on the stairs. Her heart soared.

Shade had tried to banish her from his head and failed. He'd attempted, unsuccessfully, to free his heart from her silken bonds.

And now, as he opened the apartment door and saw her standing there, between the table and the all-too-inviting feather bed, wearing only her ivory silk robe, her warm and loving heart gleaming nakedly in her eyes, Shade surrendered. To the inevitable. To Rachel.

"I give up." He held out his arms and managed a ghost of his usual rakish smile. "I'm yours, Sister Rachel. To do with as you will. For as long as you'll have me."

Seventy-two hours was not what she would have wished for. But it was more than she ever could have dreamed.

And, since she had been given no other choice, it would have to be enough. The trick was, she decided, not to waste a single second.

Laughing and crying all at the same time, she flung herself into Shade's outstretched arms.

10

SHADE KISSED RACHEL. Softly, gently, without demand, holding her as if she were the most fragile thing on earth. More breakable than the finest Irish crystal. More delicate than a hummingbird egg. He kissed her with a tenderness he'd never known he possessed, with a depth of emotion he'd never imagined himself capable of feeling.

And even as he deepened the kiss, his lips remained as soft as snowflakes. Rachel sighed with pure pleasure, parting her lips to invite the tender invasion of his tongue.

Somewhere, deep in the misty reaches of her mind, a voice—was it her own, or was it Joshua's?—warned her that what she was doing, what she was about to do, was against every tenet by which she'd been bound for all these years. But Rachel stubbornly ignored it.

Her thoughts, her body, her entire world had compressed to nothing but shimmering sensations. Her bedazzled mind was only aware of the exquisite movement of his mouth on hers, the hypnotizing touch of his hands moving up and down her back, the glorious feel of his firm male body responding to her closeness. The heavenly kiss went on and on and on. A deep-seated instinct she had not even known she possessed had her lips parting when his did. Their tongues touched.

Rachel would not have uttered a single word of complaint if it had lasted an eternity. Warmth flowed through her veins like summer sunshine, her body was leaning into his, melting irresistibly.

When Shade felt the kiss quickly drifting from pleasure to passion, he denied his own hunger and slowed the pace, determined, after all the waiting, to make this last.

Dragging his mouth away from her sweet, pliant one, he kissed first one satiny cheek, then the other. Then her eyelids. The fragrant hair at her temples.

"Lord, you are exquisite." His lips lingered at her earlobe, her throat. When his tongue created a hot wet swath along the length of her neck, she moaned softly, thrust her fingers into his dark hair and urged his mouth back to hers.

"Please." The heat within her was building, passion was threatening to flood her senses. "I need you."

Long ago, after days of torture, she'd faced her accusers and sworn never to plead for mercy from any mortal man. Three hundred years later, her oath was recklessly abandoned. Rachel would have dropped to her knees, if necessary, to beg Shade to end this exquisite torment.

What made such admission palatable was that she knew he would be willing to make the same sacrifice.

Even knowing the depth of his own feelings, which he'd been fighting against from the beginning, Rachel was unprepared for Shade's next move.

He cupped her flushed face in wide strong hands that were suspiciously unsteady. "And I need you."

His expression, the depth of emotion in his stormy green eyes told Rachel that he was not talking about a mere physical craving.

Her still-very-human heart lurched at those words, uttered so roughly, as if jerked unwillingly from between his harshly set lips.

She placed her trembling hand atop his. "I know," she whispered. Her eyes were wide and open and brimming with love.

Muttering a sound that could have been a curse or a prayer, he pulled her against him. This time the kiss was raw and powerful, shaking her to the core. Her knees weakened and, if he hadn't chosen that moment to scoop her into his arms, Rachel wasn't certain she could have continued to stand.

It was only a few feet to the bed. To Shade, the journey seemed to take a lifetime. Against every vestige of common sense he possessed, against all reason, he was desperate for this woman.

As he'd risked his life, walking through the dark and dangerous streets, sticking closely to the edges of buildings, moving through the night like a shadow, he'd tried, without any success, to understand what witchcraft Rachel Parrish possessed. What spell had she concocted that had rendered him so utterly and fatalistically defenseless against her feminine charms?

The answer to those questions had, as everything about Rachel, remained a mystery. The woman was a mystery inside a puzzle inside an enigma.

Now, as he lowered her to the mattress, Shade found himself wondering whether this craving would be satisfied after he'd finally had her. As it so often had with other women.

He stood beside the bed and began to unbutton his shirt without taking his eyes from her. She was lying on her back, gazing up at him with a combination of anticipation, trust and something else.

Fear? No, Shade concluded. Not fear. Nor apprehension. But something very close.

Anxiety? Perhaps.

Her next words confirmed his thoughts. "I don't know what to do." Her soft voice curled around him like smoke. Warmed him like good Napoleon brandy on a cold winter's night. "How to please you."

He had to smile at that. She was so grave. So earnest. So sweet. "You please me." The mattress sighed as he sat down beside her. His mouth brushed hers, at first lightly, as if seeking to reassure. Then deeper, to seduce.

Her hands slid inside his open shirt, pressing against his chest, skimming over the rugged planes of muscled flesh. Putting aside her momentary fears that Shade would find her lovemaking skills disappointing, and going solely on instinct, she pressed her lips against that hard male flesh, rewarded when he drew in a sharp breath.

Needing to touch her, as she did him, Shade untied the sash of the robe and folded the ivory silk back. Rather than the bare flesh he'd been expecting, he discovered a lacy sea-foam teddy so sheer it could have been spun from cobwebs.

When she'd first taken the scanty lingerie from its bed of white tissue paper, Rachel had been appalled at the thought of wearing anything so blatantly seductive.

But that was then. And this was now. Seeing the appreciation in Shade's green eyes, Rachel knew she'd made the right decision to throw away her whalebone corset.

"Remind me to thank Liz as soon as we get back to D.C." Shade's voice was rough. "She's one helluva shopper."

For one moment, Rachel was tempted to tell Shade the truth, that she wouldn't be returning to Washington with him. But then his mouth was on her breast and his tongue was dampening the pale green lace, creating tiny prick points of need along her skin. Thoughts spiraled away.

His fingers caressed, his mouth roamed. He kissed her breasts, her nipples. His lips created sparks along the ridge of her collarbone, down her rib cage. His mouth was hot, his hands possessive.

When he placed his palm against her mound, the heat inside her flamed so hot she was amazed the silk didn't melt. She felt a flood of moisture and gasped at the sheer pleasure of it. Her hips rose involuntarily, seeking more of this tender torment. Seeking relief.

"Shade." She tried to reach for him but her arms felt strangely heavy. "I feel . . . I need . . . Oh!" She gasped as his tongue wetly trailed down her backbone.

"Too soon." His mouth left off creating havoc at the base of her spine and returned to her parted lips. "Much, much, too soon."

He whisked the lacy teddy away, treating each bit of newly exposed flesh to his tender touch, his hot, stinging kisses. Warmth like nothing she'd ever known or could have ever imagined flowed through her as she closed her eyes and succumbed to these thrilling, unfamiliar sensations.

He murmured to her—romantic endearments, tender reassurances, impossible promises—as he kissed her throat, her ankles, the backs of her knees, the flesh she'd never known was so exquisitely sensitive. His lips and hands were everywhere, tasting, touching, tempting, arousing by irresistible degrees.

She murmured a ragged protest when he released her and left the bed to take off his own clothes. He had extremely broad shoulders and strong sinewy arms. His well-muscled chest, dusted lightly with ebony hair, gleamed bronze in the flickering candlelight.

Although it was unheard of in her day for a well-bred woman to even think of looking at a nude man, Rachel found herself unable to resist. Knowing it was wrong, knowing that such scandalous behavior was suitable more to a wanton hussy than a properly serene-minded guardian angel, she could not prevent her eyes from following that intriguing arrowing of hair downward, over his flat stomach, past the ugly scar she knew was the result of a burst appendix while he'd been camped out in the jungles of Cambodia searching for the Khmer Rouge, then lower still.

Just the sight of him took Rachel's breath away. His sex stirred with arousal, growing before her fascinated gaze.

Shade watched Rachel watching him and was reminded once again of her innocence. That she'd never seen a naked male was obvious. It was equally obvious that she was intrigued by what she was seeing.

Shade knew he was about to set the scene for the man who would come after him. The man who could offer Rachel the happily-ever-after life she deserved.

Shade hated that paragon of masculine domesticity without even knowing him. He hated the idea of Rachel looking up at any other man with such uncensored love and trust. He detested the thought of any other man kissing her, touching her, experiencing her generosity and her warmth.

And he damn well loathed the idea of any other man hearing her breathless little cries as he took her over the edge.

Shade was determined to make Rachel's first experience special. And not solely for the obvious reasons. What he wanted to do, he realized, knowing the idea to be entirely selfish and horrendously chauvinistic, what he *intended* to do was to claim Rachel as his own.

He would brand her with his mouth, his hands, so that whenever any other male dared touch her, she would feel Shade's touch instead. And if any lips ever attempted to drink from her soft sweet ones, the taste of Shade Blackstone would come between them. And when she attempted to make love to that faceless, nameless male lurking somewhere in the murky shadows of her future, Rachel would find her bed—and her body—already claimed by Shade's presence.

He returned to the bed, pulling her to him. Caught up in feelings older than the forces that had formed their universe, Rachel clung to Shade, submitting joyously to whatever he asked, allowing him to take her wherever he would.

Rachel reveled in the feathery touch of his fingers trailing through the honey-hued nest of curls at the juncture of her thighs, the tug of his teeth on a nipple, the strength of his long legs as they tangled seductively with hers.

She'd always been a realist, not given to romantic, impossible dreams. But now, for this suspended, perfect moment in time, she allowed herself to dream.

When he could take no more, when he could no longer deny the fire surging in his own loins, Shade shifted to lie on top of her, careful not to crush her.

She was so sweet. So innocent. Shade knew he didn't deserve Rachel, but that didn't stop him from wanting her. From needing her. From loving her. His lips touched hers in a soft, tender benediction as he reached between their bodies and stroked her clitoris. Damp heat flowed over his fingers. He took his shaft in his own hand and rubbed it against the ultrasensitive nub of flesh.

"I don't want to hurt you."

Her eyes fluttered open. Her hands, which had been journeying up and down his back, slowed their feverish pace. The tension inside her built as he ever so gently slipped inside her. Just barely, but enough to send her already tumultuous senses soaring.

"You could never hurt me, Shade."

When he slowly withdrew, she moaned. It was a small ragged sound, from deep in her throat.

And then, blessedly, he was back, entering her by inches, pleasuring her beyond words. "Never." Her hands framed his face; her smile was nothing short of beatific. Once again Shade was reminded of angels; once again he almost remembered where they'd met before.

The memory shimmered just out of reach, so close Shade felt as if he could reach out and touch it.

He lowered his head, touching his lips to hers as he withdrew, and then returned, repeating the tantalizing strokes until every pore in her body was screaming for release. It was torment. It was paradise.

His movements, designed to coax her to orgasm, were arousing Shade beyond anything he'd ever known. He tried to concentrate on that elusive memory, struggled to recall another time when she'd smiled at him in just that way, but his throbbing body took over his mind and he surged the rest of the way into her.

A pain stabbed into Shade as he entered her, first sharp, then sweet. She was so hot and wet and tight, he almost came instantly. Grabbing onto her hips, he held himself absolutely rigid, allowing her time to adjust to the unfamiliar invasion of her body, allowing him time to garner whatever tattered remnants remained of his self-control.

And then he began to move, withdrawing almost all the way, then returning even deeper. After the first shuddering shock, Rachel began to move, as well. Her short unpainted fingernails dug into the flesh of his back, her legs wrapped around his lean hips as she clasped him tighter, begging him with words and motions not to stop now. Not to leave her on this terrifying, thrilling precipice.

He felt her hot, ragged breath against his neck. Felt the sting of her nails, the straining, taut muscles of her thighs. Her body was pulsing around him, massaging his burning sex as they moved with a shared harmony that was heartbreakingly painful in its perfection.

They took each other higher and higher. Together, they crested the shimmering peak, soaring for a thrillingly long time. Finally, hands clasped, lips touching, they drifted back to earth, where their earlier urgency was replaced by a sweetness all its own.

They lay that way for a long, silent time, their arms, legs and hearts entwined. "I love you." Shade's words, spoken solemnly in the stillness of the room, were the answer to all Rachel's unspoken prayers. They brought more joy than she ever could have believed possible. And more pain.

"And I love you," she whispered.

Her tone did not reveal the pleasure Shade would have expected. He glanced down, stricken by the sheen of tears brightening her remarkable silver eyes. "You don't sound all that happy."

It wasn't that there wouldn't be problems, Shade admitted. But they were two intelligent, capable individuals. Surely they could work out whatever glitches such an abrupt change in agenda might present.

"I am." She gave him a wobbly little smile that did nothing to ease the cold hand that had begun to squeeze his heart. "Really."

Early warning bells were tolling. All Shade's instincts were telling him that once again Rachel was not revealing the truth. But feeling too mellow to argue at the moment, he decided to put the problem aside. For now.

After all, he tried to reassure himself as he extricated himself from her embrace, she'd had a long and trying time delivering that baby. Perhaps it was only exhaustion that had her behaving so strangely.

"I'll be right back." He brushed his lips against hers and left the bed. Rachel squeezed her eyes tight and vowed not to cry. She'd just experienced the most exquisite, thrilling lovemaking any woman from any century could have hoped for. The man responsible for that had just told her he loved her. Unnecessarily, since his hands and mouth and body had demonstrated that, but it was, Rachel decided, nice to hear the words.

She'd been given more than many women were blessed with in several lifetimes. So why was she feeling so horribly bereft?

Because she'd also discovered one more thing about herself she'd never known. She was a greedy woman. She wanted more than just this stolen time apart with Shade. She wanted tomorrow. More than that, she wanted all their tomorrows.

What she wanted, she realized bleakly, was forever.

It was also impossible.

Shade found her lying on her back, her arm over her eyes, looking small and frail and heartbreakingly vulnerable. He knew he'd hurt her, albeit briefly, knew it couldn't be helped, but he also knew that after that initial pain, she'd gone on to enjoy herself.

Despite all the missing facts about her life, Shade had come to know Rachel well enough to know when she was lying. And her orgasm definitely hadn't been faked.

"Whatever it is that's bothering you can't be all that bad," he suggested quietly. The mattress dipped as he sat down beside her, sending her sliding against his bare leg.

Rachel removed her arm and looked up at him, her eyes as unpromisingly bleak as her expression. "That's what you say now."

"Answer me one thing." He began soothing her deflowered flesh with the warm wet towel. When he viewed the dark stains on the soft flesh at the inside of her thighs, he felt a stab of guilt along with an unmistakable surge of masculine possession. Rachel was his. For now. Forever.

"Anything." Her frank answer, the first since he'd known her, surprised Shade. He took one look at her face and knew she meant it.

"You're not here to kill me, are you?"

"Of course not!" Her eyes widened, not with pleasure, but shock that he'd even suggest such a thing. After what they'd just shared.

"I didn't think so." When he brushed the towel over the swollen pink bud, Rachel flinched. "I'm sorry. I didn't mean to hurt you."

"Actually," she admitted on a nervous little laugh, "pain had very little to do with what I just felt."

Shade laughed. "You are," he murmured against her smiling lips, "the most incredibly responsive woman I've ever met."

His stroking touch between her legs, meant solely to soothe, was arousing her anew. "I am, aren't I?" Her soft voice was tinged with a beguiling blend of wonder and feminine pride.

"Absolutely." Although Shade's body was reacting painfully to her uncensored response, he reminded himself that taking her again, so soon, would be unreasonably selfish. "Are you hungry?"

"Hungry?" It was difficult to think when his lips were plucking so enticingly at hers and that delicious heat was building yet again between her legs.

"For food. From the table you set, it looks as if Burke's cook went all out."

She glanced over at the food she'd completely forgotten. "She did. And I suppose I could eat something." Her tone indicated it was not her first choice, either.

"What would you say to smoked pheasant and caviar in bed?"

"I'd say it sounds horribly decadent."

He winked and gave her another quick, hard kiss. "That's the idea."

He left the bed and went over to the table. It was the first time she'd seen his naked back close up. Rachel was aghast.

"Oh, my God," she cried.

He spun toward the door, half-expecting to find the general's entire secret-police squad standing there with machine guns. He had already retrieved his pistol from the table when he realized that Rachel's look of horror was directed at him.

"Your back," she murmured in explanation. She shouldn't be surprised. After all, she'd been forced to witness the terror the general's men had inflicted on Shade. But to see those horrid scars in person . . .

Shade shrugged. "They're only scars, Rachel. Nothing to get so upset about." Unwilling to discuss those hellish days with her so soon after experiencing heaven, Shade turned back to the table and began slicing the pheasant.

Rachel slipped from the bed and went over to stand behind him. "I hate him," she whispered hotly as she ran her palms over Shade's shoulders and forced herself to look unflinchingly at the vivid proof of the general's evil soul.

Those wide shoulders moved in another shrug beneath her hands. "Well, you're not alone there."

Hate was forbidden in Rachel's peaceful realm. Another rule broken. With scant regret.

"I hate him for this." She pressed her lips against one long, ragged welt that snaked from his shoulder to his hip. "For this." She kissed a row of round white circles she knew to be the result of a lit cigar. "And this." Another jagged line, white rather than red, but just as ugly.

His broad back was covered with the red and white lines, a virtual road map of the tortures he'd survived. He stood there, his fingers curved around the edge of the table, as Rachel kissed every one. "Someday he'll pay for this."

Never had any woman treated him with such an outpouring of love. "He will. In spades," Shade agreed gruffly. "But, if you don't mind, sweetheart, I'd rather not talk about that bastard right now."

When he turned, took her in his arms and shared another of those long, wonderful kisses that made her toes curl, Rachel decided he was right.

Fate had granted them this stolen time together. It would be wrong to allow such a horrid man as the general into their magical realm.

He released her, then spread the glossy black caviar onto a cracker and held it out to her. "Gotta keep your strength up. We still have another twenty-four hours before we leave for the compound."

Another twenty-four hours. Well, it wasn't the lifetime she'd wished for. But it would be enough, Rachel vowed. It would have to be.

"We'll have to spend such time wisely," she suggested after she'd finished chewing. The caviar was definitely better than it looked.

"Of course." He filled a plate with various goodies and walked the short distance with her back to the bed. "Any ideas?"

She cocked her head, listening to the gunfire she hadn't heard while making love. "I suppose it's too dangerous to go sight-seeing."

"Absolutely." He handed her a glass of wine.

She sipped the ruby cabernet as Shade piled slices of pheasant onto freshly baked French bread. "And there's no electricity, so the television won't work."

"That eliminates spending the day watching soaps," he said agreeably. "Or playing 'Wheel of Fortune.'" Besides, he thought, gazing at the naked nymph sitting cross-legged amid the love-rumpled sheets, he'd already spun that fickle wheel and come up a grand prize winner.

"True." She nodded solemnly as she allowed him to feed her another bite of caviar. "I suppose we'll just have to rely on our imaginations."

"Sister Rachel," he said with a bold, rakish grin, "that is, by far, the best idea you've come up with yet."

They continued to share the wine and eat the excellent meal in comfortable harmony. By mutual unspoken agreement, they kept their conversation to happy topics: the baby they'd delivered together, the special pleasure of waking up on a winter morning and discovering the world wearing a soft cape of pristine white snow, the joy of seeing a brilliant rainbow after a late summer thunderstorm.

Shade told her all about his house, including the bit about the raccoons, which made her laugh, as it had Marianne. Immersed in the sheer enjoyment of being with the woman he loved, Shade failed to notice that Rachel, as usual, told him nothing about herself.

Later, physically satiated and happier than he'd ever thought he had a right to be, Shade drew her down beside him and wrapped his arms around her. And then they slept. The peaceful, unfretful sleep of innocents.

When Shade awoke, he found her gone. Cursing, he sat bolt upright and reached for the pistol he'd placed on the floor beside the bed, just in case.

And then he saw her sitting in a chair by the shuttered window. She'd gotten dressed again, which he thought was both a disappointment and a waste of time. Since he had every intention of stripping that T-shirt and tight jeans off her.

He was picturing the enjoyment of doing precisely that when her expression stopped him cold. Ice skimmed up his spine. The hairs at the back of his neck prickled.

"There's something I have to tell you."

He'd been waiting for days for Rachel to open up. And now, finally, it appeared she was ready. Unfortunately, from her flat tone and the regret he viewed in those remarkable gray eyes, Shade had the feeling he wasn't going to like what Rachel was about to reveal. Not even a little bit.

He was right. What Shade had no way of knowing, not yet, was that what Rachel was about to say would turn his entire world, as he'd always known it, upside down.

Years of practice allowed him to keep his own expression inscrutable, his voice steady.

"It's about time."

11

SHADE STARED AT HER.

He'd known Rachel was an enigma. He hadn't realized she was crazy. She certainly didn't act like a nut case. But from what she'd been telling him for the past twenty-five minutes, it was obvious that the luscious lady either had one hell of an imagination or was one taco short of a combination plate.

"Let me get this straight," he said in a calm tone designed not to set off the crazy lady. "You believe you're an angel."

"I *am* an angel," she corrected quietly.

"A guardian angel." He'd thrown on a pair of jeans and his shirt—not bothering to button it—before she'd begun her story. Now, still barefoot, he began pacing in long strides.

She nodded, pleased he was proving so accepting. She'd feared, knowing Shade's cynical outlook on life, that convincing him would prove difficult. "That's right. I'm your guardian angel."

"Yeah. That's what you said. Along with all those other guys."

"I've had quite a few assignments. But I've been with you since—"

"The day I was born," he broke in. "I was given to you by your boss, Jeremy something-or-other."

"Joshua."

"That's right, Joshua. The former actor. The guy I saw in the restaurant."

So he had seen them together. Rachel was not surprised. "I warned Joshua he was taking a risk approaching me in public that way."

"Yeah. His wings could have caught on fire from all the candles on the tables."

When Rachel chose not to respond to his sarcasm, Shade raked a frustrated hand through his hair. "And before you were an angel, you were a witch."

"I wasn't a witch." Both her tone and her back stiffened. "I was a midwife."

"In Salem. In 1692."

"Yes. I know it's a little difficult to take in, all at one time, but—"

"How about impossible?"

He was honestly sorry that Rachel had such serious mental problems. But he was getting tired of this game, tired of humoring her when what she needed was a lot of therapy, and some heavy pharmaceuticals.

"Nevertheless," Rachel continued, "it is all true. I *was* a midwife. But I made the mistake of adopting a new method of childbirth. Rather than the traditional method of tying a woman's hands to the bed frame and giving her a birthing stick to chew on during contractions, I advocated breathing exercises."

"Natural childbirth isn't exactly new."

"It was in 1692," Rachel pointed out evenly. "You have to understand, Shade, Puritan Salem was a very rigidly controlled society."

"So I've read."

"Any new ideas were suspect. New ideas from a mere female, well . . ." She shrugged her shoulders.

"So when your fiancé, the Reverend Dimmesdale—"

"Demming," she corrected quietly. Even after all these centuries, her former beloved's betrayal still hurt. "Roger's name was Demming."

Shade ground his teeth. "So, when *Roger* found out what you were doing, he turned you over to the council."

"He believed I had come under Satan's influence. As a minister, he had no choice but to save the rest of the community from my supposed moral corruption."

That was it. Shade stopped pacing long enough to squat in front of her and take her hands, which were, he noted, ice-cold in both of his. "Rachel. Sweetheart," he coaxed, "do you have any idea how impossible all this sounds?"

Her gaze was solemn. And immeasurably sad. "Do you have any idea how impossible it felt? To be accused of such things by the man you had planned to marry from childhood? To be subjected to such horribly personal interrogation."

Her voice had risen, she'd begun to tremble. "Do you have any idea how it feels to be ridiculed. Then scorned. Then ultimately..."

Now her entire body was encased in a block of ice and her eyes were no longer focused on his face but were looking past him into the dark and horrible nightmare of her tortured past.

No, Shade corrected, not her past. Only her tortured mind.

"The smoke from the torches burned my eyes," she whispered tremblingly. "And there was thunder. And lightning. Then Roger put the rope around my neck and—"

"That's enough, dammit!" He took hold of her shoulders and shook her. Hard. "It didn't happen, Rachel. There wasn't a trial, there were no torches. There wasn't any rope. You didn't hang. You're here, with me."

Her gaze returned to the present. To Shade. "I know where I am. And who I'm with. I also know where I have been. And where I am from."

"Now we're back to heaven."

"Some people call it that."

"What do you call it?"

"Home."

The single word was spoken with absolute conviction. Not that what she was saying was possible, he reminded himself. But it was readily apparent that she believed her out-of-this-world story to be the truth. In that respect she wasn't a great deal different from all those people who believed themselves to have been beamed up from cornfields by alien spaceships, he decided.

"So why don't you tell me about home?"

"All right." She was about to break another rule, but special circumstances, Rachel reminded herself, called for special actions. "I will."

But as she attempted to describe her more recent life, she found her memory strangely fogged, as if she were recalling some distant dream.

"I can't," she admitted finally.

"Now why aren't I surprised?"

"You don't have to be so sarcastic."

"If you're really an angel, where are your wings?"

"We don't have wings. That's merely artistic interpretation. And as attractive as they appear in all those paintings, it has always seemed to me they'd be highly impractical."

"Can't have impracticality in heaven," he drawled.

Rachel knew he didn't believe her. Though she was sorely tempted to drop the subject and spend the scant time they had on earth together at more pleasurable pursuits, she couldn't do it.

If nothing else, she knew how much it had cost Shade to admit that he loved her. When she was gone—and about this she had no choice—she wanted him to believe that she had loved him back. With ever fiber of her being. She couldn't bear the idea that he'd believe her capable of abandoning him. As his mother had so many years ago.

"One of those scars on your back was not caused by the general's men," she said, trying yet again to prove her case. "A woman stabbed you. A double agent you were working with in Germany."

"You could have found that in my files."

"Does it say in those files that the injury was sustained in the shower?"

His eyes hardened. As did his jaw. Shade gave her a long, probing look. "No. But there were people who knew the truth." Like the woman's cohorts who'd succeeded in bugging the supposed safe house. After the incident, Shade had viewed the videotape. It hadn't been pretty.

Rachel took a deep breath and tried again. And again. But every time she revealed knowledge about his various dangerous, near-death experiences, he countered she could have gotten the information from his government files.

"All right. If this doesn't prove my claim, I don't know what will." She sighed and folded her hands together in her lap. "One Christmas, when you were eleven, you and Conlan became blood brothers. It snowed that day. Conlan was wearing blue, you wore gray.

"Afterward, you both returned to the hockey game. You were a strong skater, the best player on the team. You trapped the puck with your stick, then took off across the lake."

Shade remembered the December wind howling in his ears; the snow had been falling in a thick white curtain, obscuring his vision. He imagined he could hear the sound of the fragile ice giving way beneath the serrated steel runners of his skates.

"You fell through the ice."

"The accident is undoubtedly in my school files," he argued. "If you knew where to look." His voice, even to his own ears, lacked its earlier strong conviction.

"You didn't give up," Rachel continued softly, as if she hadn't heard his rebuttal. "You kept searching for an escape route."

"But I couldn't find one." The day, long forgotten, came flooding back.

"No. And when you couldn't, you realized you were going to die."

Their minds linked, both focused on that long-ago day.

"And then I saw her," Shade murmured. Reality slammed home, like a fist to the jaw. He stared unbelievingly at Rachel. "Swimming toward me, surrounded by a warm golden light. At first I thought she was a mermaid, but that didn't make any sense.

"Her hair was streaming behind her and her eyes were as gray as the ice overhead, but I remember knowing, when I looked into them, that I was going to be all right."

"And you were."

"Yes." He dragged his hands through his hair again and realized they were shaking. "Everything went black about then. But later, back at the infirmary, even when I was telling myself that my mermaid had been a hallucination, I felt something brush against my cheek and I knew."

Silent tears made silver ribbons down Rachel's cheeks. "That you weren't alone."

"Yes." With trembling fingers he reached out and brushed the moisture away. "My God," he rasped, "I remember it all so clearly. It was you." He shook his head in one last try at denial. "But that's impossible."

"Nothing's impossible."

Shade had not lived an uneventful life. He'd thought there was nothing left that could surprise him. He'd been wrong.

"I thought from the beginning you reminded me of an angel, but this is ridiculous."

Her smile, as she framed his frowning face between her soft palms, gave him an insider's glimpse of the heaven he'd never believed in.

"You made me a woman," she reminded him.

Her lips were only a whisper away, inviting him to paradise. But old images, learned in the chapel of the rigidly run Calvinist boys' school, died hard.

"Hell, Rachel, you can't expect me to accept the wild idea that you're an angel, then be able to, well, you know, be that way with you ever again."

"Be what way?" She brushed her smiling mouth against his teasingly. Tantalizingly. "This way?" One hand slid down his neck, across his shoulders, settling against his bare chest. Her lips followed. "This way?" she whispered. Beneath her mouth, his heart trebled its beat. The sound of his zipper lowering was unnervingly loud in the suspended hush surrounding them. "How about this way?"

Her lips continued their sensual, erotic journey as Rachel proved to Shade that they could, indeed, still be *that way* together.

And as the hours passed, each time, in every way, their lovemaking grew more exquisite. More profound.

Because it was an expression of a love so deep and so strong it transcended the normal realms of time and space.

IT WAS TIME FOR their meeting with the general. Luck appeared to be with them as they drove to the village of Karikistan without running into any more sniper fire.

Unfortunately, Rachel still had not accomplished her mission: to keep Shade from assassinating the general. Because though she argued heatedly against his plan during the drive away from the city, she could not lessen his resolve.

"You cannot kill another human being," she argued for at least the tenth time in as many minutes.

"I have. And I can."

"You've never committed murder," she said, reminding Shade once again that Rachel knew him as well as he knew himself.

"He deserves to die."

"That's probably true," she surprised him by agreeing. "But it's not your place."

He shrugged. "If not me, then who?" He shot her a sideways glance as they drove to the square in the middle of the village, where they were to meet the general's guards. "You?"

"Of course not!" She may have broken a great many rules during her brief time on earth, but some commandments remained inviolate.

"Then I guess it's up to me." He reached over and patted her on the knee. "Besides, don't forget, I've got an ace in the hole."

"And that is?"

"You." His brief smile lacked the warmth she'd grown accustomed to during these love-filled hours. "It never hurts to have pull in high places." This time his smile almost, but not quite, reached his eyes. "And if you're telling the truth, we're talking about as high as a person can get."

"You still don't believe me."

"I don't want to." A shadow moved across those unsmiling eyes. "But I'll have to admit, angel, you've definitely piqued my interest."

She sighed. It had seemed so easy in the beginning. Make a brief sojourn to earth, save Shade's soul, then return to work, as she had so many years ago after pulling him from that icy grave. Unfortunately, nothing about Shade was proving to be simple, least of all her feelings for the man.

"You know," she insisted, "you're not nearly as bad as you think you are."

"Nor nearly as good as you think I am," he countered.

She opened her mouth to argue, when she saw the armored personnel vehicle blocking the roadway up ahead. "Looks as if we've reached our destination." Shade retrieved his hand from her knee and returned it to the steering wheel. His expression was calm, but Rachel couldn't help noticing that he was gripping the wheel so hard his knuckles had turned white.

Shade left the car and spoke with one of the guards, who insisted Rachel get out, as well. The stars on his shoulder attested to his high rank. His expression, as he instructed his men to check Rachel for hidden weapons, attested to his cruelty.

From the way he was watching Shade watch the man whose hands moved intimately over her body, Rachel knew that the soldier was waiting, hoping, even, for Shade to make a move so he could respond with brute force.

"I'm sorry," Shade said after the search was completed and they were back in the car.

"There wasn't anything you could do without risking getting us both killed."

"I know. But when that bastard's hands—"

It was her turn to place her hand on his knee. "Don't think about it. He didn't hurt me."

"I wanted to kill him." A muscle jerked ominously in his jaw.

"But you didn't." And for that, Rachel was immensely grateful.

"No." This time his smile revealed the warmth his earlier ones had been missing. "Maybe you're right, Sister Rachel. Perhaps I'm not quite the hired gun I pretend to be."

"You're the man I love."

In the beginning, that idea had proven even more unbelievable than her claim about being his guardian angel. Never, in all his thirty-plus years had Shade ever thought of himself as the least bit lovable.

"And you're the lady I love." He covered her hand with his and linked their fingers together. "Forever."

"Do you love me enough to do one thing for me?"

Her innocent tone didn't fool him for a second. Shade cursed. "Like forgoing the pleasure of killing the general?"

"Yes."

"Exactly like living with Jiminy Cricket," he muttered, repeating his earlier accusation. "How about I promise to think about it?"

It was a start. Rachel's heart soared hopefully. "That would make me very happy."

"Once this is over and we've got Conlan out of the country, I'm going to spend the rest of our lives making you happy."

It was a promise Rachel knew Shade would never be able to keep. But, unwilling to ruin their brief time together, she'd not told him of her deadline, so she could not mention it now.

"You always make me happy," she murmured instead.

They followed the procession of armored trucks to the compound located approximately five kilometers outside the village.

Inside a former farmhouse, surrounded by heavily armed guards, they found the general. "Hello, Shade," the older man greeted his enemy with a smile that belied the torture that had taken place last time the two men had met. "I had not expected to see you again."

"You know what they say about bad pennies," Shade drawled, ignoring the man's outstretched hand.

The insult hit home. Rachel watched the red flush rise from the collar of the man's olive drab fatigues. Just when she thought General Rutskoya was going to respond harshly to Shade's lack of protocol, he turned toward her.

"Ms. Parrish." His bow was low and continental, designed to impress. "If Shade's usual traveling companions were even half as lovely as you, he would be more than welcome in my country anytime."

His dark eyes made her flesh crawl. "Thank you, General. That's very kind."

"And you're very beautiful." Rutskoya's gaze moved from the top of her honey-blond head over her body, clad in a black jersey cat suit. The outfit had been designed for ease of movement. It also showed off every feminine curve.

"I thought we were going to talk business," Shade said. He began to slip his hands into his pockets to keep them from curving around the bastard's neck. When the gesture drew a quick response from the general's bodyguards, he dropped his hands to his sides instead.

"All in good time, my friend," the general counseled.

Shade was in no mood to be patient. Conlan was still imprisoned and the general's beady dark eyes were undressing Shade's woman. Enough was enough.

"Look. If you don't want the damn guns, just let me know and I'll be on my way. Thanks to the celebrated New World Order turning out to be armed chaos, I've got buyers all over three continents."

"Too true," the general agreed. He gave Rachel one long last look, then returned his attention to Shade. "I must admit, Shade, that I was surprised you'd turned to such unsavory endeavors."

"It wasn't like I was exactly a Boy Scout in my previous life. Besides, after your goons finished with me, the government put me out to pasture."

"I heard you became a mercenary."

"A guy's got to eat. Besides, I'm not cut out for retirement. Two days of fishing and I'm itching for action."

"If it's action you are looking for," the general suggested, "you've come to the right place."

"That's what I heard."

General Rutskoya wasn't going to be a pushover. Watching him carefully studying Shade, Rachel understood how the man had achieved so much unquestioned power. He was brutal, yes, but he was also intelligent.

"I find it difficult to believe you would want to do business with me. After our history."

"What's past is past," Shade said with a negligent shrug. "I did my job infiltrating your army. Your job was to make me pay when you caught me. No point in getting personal."

The general threw back his head and laughed. A big, booming laugh that had the other men in the room exchanging smiles. The tension eased.

"Tell me what you are selling," Rutskoya said, finally getting down to business.

The meeting continued for three long and wearying hours, during which time the general's aides brought wine, pots of tea and thick sandwiches piled high with meats and cheeses. The rest of the people in Yaznovia might be starving, but the meal, even more than the weapons, proved all too clearly that rank did, indeed, have its privileges.

"All right," the general said finally, rising to his feet. "I believe our collaboration will prove equally beneficial. When can you provide delivery?"

Once again Shade refused to accept the extended hand. "As soon as Conlan is released, I'll call my contact in Montacroix and the shipment will be driven across the border."

The general rubbed his chin. "You drive a hard bargain, my friend."

"It's Conlan for the guns. That's my bottom line."

"As it so happens, your friend is currently here, in the compound prison," the general revealed, not telling Shade anything he didn't already know. "If you can arrange to have the weapons at the border by noon tomorrow, your friend will be released then."

"Deal." Finally Shade shook the general's hand. "They'll be there. At noon on the dot." By then he, Rachel and Conlan should be out of the country. Shade turned to Rachel. "Let's go." He took hold of her arm and together they walked toward the door.

"Just one minute." The general's words stopped them in their tracks.

"Forget something?" Shade asked conversationally over his shoulder.

"Where are you staying?"

"Back at the village."

"Perhaps you would care to remain here, in order to avoid the drive."

There was no way he was going to willingly stay under this man's roof. Not after what he'd been through the last time he'd been the general's unwilling guest.

"It's only five kilometers," Shade pointed out.

"True. But I was thinking that perhaps Ms. Parrish would care to join me for dinner. We have a very fine chef here at the compound," he said, directing his words to Rachel. "The man does wonders with roast lamb."

The fact that he was omitting Shade from the invitation told Rachel that his plans had nothing to do with a desire to show off his cook's culinary skills.

She forced what she hoped was a winning albeit regretful smile. "That's very kind, but—"

Shade's fingers tightened imperceptibly. "The lady's allergic to lamb. She also has plans for the evening."

It was obvious the general was less than pleased by Shade's possessive attitude. But as if he were afraid of blowing the arms deal over a mere woman, he dropped the issue.

"Tomorrow then," he said tightly. "Ten o'clock."

"Tomorrow," Shade agreed.

THEY PLANNED TO SPEND the night at a small inn, which Shade revealed was owned by a member of the partisan underground who'd been doing their best to unseat the general. It did not escape Rachel's notice that both the elderly man and his plump country wife treated Shade like a returning hero.

"You're certainly popular around here," she murmured after she and Shade were alone in their comfortable but rustic room.

"Zdeslav and Duha are old friends. Without their help I probably would have died in that prison."

"How helpful was Franja?"

"Franja?"

"Zdeslav and Duha's daughter." Rachel had been amazed at the jolt of jealousy that had surged through her when the voluptuous young woman had thrown her arms around Shade's neck and kissed him. Smack on the lips! "You know, the woman who could have played a starring role in all those dirty jokes about farmers' daughters."

Shade stopped closing the shutters and glanced at her, surprised by her unusually gritty tone. "I didn't realize they had dirty jokes in 1692."

She waved her hand dismissively. "There have always been farmers. And daughters. And you haven't answered my question."

"Are you jealous?" Shade rather liked the idea.

"Horribly," she admitted on a shaky little laugh. She could no more deny those unfamiliar, unsettling feelings than she could sprout those wings he'd accused her of having.

He chuckled and drew her into his arms. "Join the club," he said against her hair. "Because I just about go ballistic every time I see any man even look at you sideways."

"I was afraid you were going to hit the general."

"You and me both, angel." His lips trailed down her throat as his hands got busy on the buttons of her sweater.

His touch was already making her knees weak. "I thought we had plans."

"We do." His fingers dispensed with the front clasp of her bra with a quick flick. "Several of them." He dipped his head, absorbing her sweet taste as his tongue skimmed across her pale flesh and teased a taut nipple. "And making love with you is at the top of the list."

Music, sweet and haunting, filled her head even as weakness engulfed her body. "But we have to rescue Conlan."

She was so sweet. "And we will." He unfastened her jeans and slid his hand inside, cupping her warmth in his palm. "But we can't break into the compound until it's dark. Which gives us, I figure, at least three hours to kill."

"You're so very clever," she gasped as a long finger slipped beneath the elastic leg band of her bikini underpants. "I suppose that's why you're the boss."

"Got it." He touched her in the way he'd discovered she loved to be touched, in the way that could send her soaring.

Rachel clung to him. Her fingers dug into his shoulders and she cried out as her spirit seemed to fly from her body, then shatter into a thousand crystalline pieces.

When she'd returned to earth, when she could breathe again, they resumed undressing each other, laughing at stubborn buttons, Shade swearing lightly at stuck zippers. They moved to the bed, where Shade marveled at the wonder of this woman he'd come to love more than he'd ever dreamed possible. Her slender limbs intrigued him, her curves were a delight. He wanted to touch, to savor, to taste, every glorious inch.

In turn, Rachel grew absolutely giddy as she reveled in the play of smooth muscle beneath the dark warm flesh and thrilled to his hot male taste.

The brisk Alpine air outside grew colder; inside, the room practically glowed from a warmth of their own making. Power shifted as the shadows on the white-washed walls grew longer. Rachel discovered that the more she gave, the more she received, while Shade learned that surrender did not always mean defeat.

Emotions, deeper than the deepest river, poured out of him and into her. Feelings, glorious, gilded feelings, flowed out of her and into him. Urgency gave way to tenderness, which in turn gave way to love.

Their hands linked. Watching each other, loving each other, they joined—bodies, minds and souls. And the absolute glory of their shared release made Rachel weep.

12

THERE WAS A NEW MOON that night. In addition, Mother Nature pitched in to help, providing a low cloud cover that prevented any starlight from brightening the general's compound.

Dressed in the olive drab uniforms of the general's guards, Shade and Rachel made their way stealthily to the prison. Although Rachel had tucked her blond hair inside her cap and was wearing an oversized, long-sleeved shirt and baggy trousers, there had been little they could do to conceal her feminine curves.

"How do you know your friend will show up?" Rachel asked softly.

"He will." He'd better, Shade amended silently.

Because if the partisan who'd infiltrated the general's troops didn't follow through on his part of the plan, Shade and Rachel would be up that proverbial creek without a paddle.

There had been a time when Shade had willingly taken such risks without giving all that much thought to the consequences. But that was before Rachel. Before he had anyone besides himself to worry about. Before he had any real reason to survive, anything or anyone to live for. Despite her apparent honesty, and even though somehow, she knew about that long-ago winter's day when he'd fallen through the ice, Shade still couldn't buy Rachel's story.

Oh, he had no doubt that she was an angel. After all, he'd thought that from the beginning. But she was, most definitely, the flesh-and-blood kind. And what he felt for her was a very long way from spiritual.

Put simply and directly, he loved her. Enough that he was willing to give up the only life he'd ever known. The solitary existence of a loner. In fact, though he hadn't found the right moment to broach the subject to Rachel, Shade had decided that as soon as they returned Conlan safe and sound to Marianne in D.C., he intended to take Rachel to Vermont, where they would spend the rest of their lives watching the grass grow and listening to the birds sing. And making babies.

Amazingly, he even wanted a family with Rachel. As they slipped through the shadows, Shade thought about all the times they'd made love these past two and a half days and wondered if perhaps, even now, she was carrying their child inside her. The idea gave him an extraordinary amount of pleasure.

That idea brought up another terrifying one. What if he couldn't keep her safe from harm tonight? Naturally he'd tried to order her to remain behind at the inn, where Zdeslav and Duha could keep an eye on her.

But, unsurprisingly, she'd refused. She was the most frustratingly stubborn person—male or female—he'd ever met. Shade decided that if by any chance her wild story about a celestial life was true, he knew why God was always pictured as an old man. Trying to reason with Rachel Parrish on a daily basis would undoubtedly turn any man gray.

They'd reached the heavily barred outer door. Shade knocked. Once. Twice. Then a third time in the prearranged code. The door swung open, the squeaky hinges sounding like a screech in the silent night.

Shade cursed inwardly as a dog patrolling the perimeter of the compound barked. The damn door should have been oiled. If such a foolish mistake cost Rachel her life . . .

"You made it," said the man who'd opened the door. He looked at Rachel with obvious surprise. "I thought you'd be alone."

"My plans changed at the last minute."

"Whatever." The man shrugged. "Here are the keys. Your friend is on the lower level. In the far cell block." He handed Shade a roughly drawn map.

"We'll find it." Shade shook the guard's hand. "Thanks."

"Just get the good doctor out," the man said. "Before they kill him."

With those less than encouraging words ringing in their ears, Shade and Rachel made their way down the dungeon hallways. The air in the prison was cold and rank. Yellow overhead lights cast flickering shadows on the damp stone walls. The only sounds were the scratching of rats in dark corners, the creaking of overhead timbers and the low moans from unseen men locked away in cramped, filthy cells. As they descended the stairway to the bowels of the prison, Shade broke out in an involuntary sweat. The place brought back memories too painful to ever entirely put behind him. He knew that, were he to close his eyes, he would see his torturers' faces, feel the sting of the whip and the electric prod that made his blood boil in his veins.

He also knew that, were he to live another hundred years, he would not forget the sound of the general's laughter as he'd writhed helplessly on the damp stone floor.

The bastard deserved to die. And during those long weeks of unrelenting torture, Shade had vowed that someday he would be the man to send the general to hell.

Which was exactly where the man belonged. The problem was, since falling in love with Rachel, his resolve had begun to crumble. It wasn't that he'd have any trouble killing Rutskoya. But if he did follow through with his original plan, he wasn't certain he could live with the disappointment he'd see in Rachel's eyes every time she looked at him.

Rachel's love versus his long-sought-after revenge. He weighed the choices, knowing, deep down inside, that he could not have both.

The dilemma was still unresolved when he suddenly heard the sound of a match being struck, followed by the smell of phosphorus, then smoke.

Grabbing hold of Rachel's wrist, he yanked her back around the corner, pressed her tight against the wall and put a warning finger against her lips. He'd taken his automatic pistol from his belt and unfastened the safety.

She nodded calmly though her eyes had widened with fear. She had a right to be afraid, Shade knew. If they were caught and she was taken prisoner...

No! He would not even allow himself to consider the possibility of his angel falling into Rutskoya's brutal hands. He would keep her safe, Shade vowed. After all, he intended to spend the rest of his life with this woman.

He had the advantage of surprise. There'd be time to get off two shots. That would be all he needed.

The guards' voices grew closer, echoing in the cavernous underground compound. Rachel's back was up against the damp, mossy wall, Shade's chest was pressed against hers.

Even this close, she could not see his face. But she knew his green eyes would be offering her reassurance. And love. Such knowledge helped her stay calm even as her nerves were stretched to the breaking point.

And then, blessedly, the guards turned another corner, headed in the opposite direction. When she heard their laughter fading, Rachel looked upward in gratitude. She had no doubt that their sudden change in direction was Joshua's doing.

Shade waited another long minute. Then nodded. He and Rachel continued past the rows of cell blocks until they came to an isolated one far from the others.

"It's time for reveille," Shade said softly, speaking for the first time since they'd entered the prison. The man lying in a fetal position on the floor struggled to sit up. Clad in filthy rags, he appeared frightfully thin. His dirty blond hair hung lankily almost to his shoulders, his face was swollen and covered with bruises. His nose had obviously been broken. But when he smiled, a bold, swashbuckling grin that lacked a top front tooth, Rachel realized that Conlan O'Donahue was a very handsome man.

"It's about time you showed up."

"What's the matter?" Shade asked. "Don't tell me you're getting bored here at club Rutskoya." His tone was flip but his voice was husky with emotion.

"The food stinks and the recreational activities aren't all they're cracked up to be in the brochures." Con looked at Rachel with obvious surprise. "Hello."

"Hello." They studied each other while Shade unlocked the cell door. "Marianne sends her love."

"You know my wife?"

"Not well, but I did spend the night at your house—"

"When? How is she?" Conlan struggled to stand up, but one leg crumpled and he fell back to the stone floor. "Does she know where I am?"

"We can catch you up on all the news of home later," Shade said. He entered the cell and lifted his best friend to his feet. "First, let's get the hell out of here."

Rachel rushed forward to offer support, and together the three of them made their way out of the cell, headed back in the direction she and Shade had just come. Although the tunnels twisted and turned like a labyrinth, Rachel had the feeling that they were nearing the stairs.

She was right. Unfortunately, as they turned the last corner, standing in front of them was General Rutskoya, flanked by a trio of armed guards.

"Hello, Shade." Looking amazingly calm, he was smoking a cigar. "Ms. Parrish." His gaze flicked over her with obvious disapproval. "I much prefer the outfit you were wearing this afternoon, my dear. In the future I shall expect more effort from you."

His implication hung between them. Rachel felt Shade stiffen beside her and prayed that he wouldn't do anything foolish.

Rutskoya's attention turned to Conlan. "You disappoint me, Dr. O'Donahue. Does your leaving so unexpectedly mean that you haven't enjoyed your visit?"

"You know what they say about guests overstaying their welcome," Con quipped with a sarcasm that allowed Rachel, for the first time, to understand how much Conlan O'Donahue and Shade had in common. They were both absolutely fearless.

The general was obviously not amused. His eyes hardened to obsidian, his mouth drew into a tight, dangerous line. "I must ask you to hand over your weapon, Shade."

Shade cursed but did as ordered. He'd been called rash in his day, but he wasn't about to attempt a reenactment of the shoot-out at the O.K. corral when he was outgunned four to one.

"I'm sorry, Shade," Conlan murmured. Shade's only response was a shrug. Then, to Rachel's surprise, he released his hold on his friend. Despite the fact that he'd obviously lost a great deal of weight, Con still outweighed Rachel by at least fifty pounds. When she was unable to support him by herself, he folded to the ground at the general's feet.

Without blinking an eye, another guard pulled his foot back, prepared to slam a booted toe into Conlan's ribs.

All hell broke loose. With a roar, Conlan rolled into the guard's shins, knocking him to the floor. Conlan immediately jumped on top of him, relieving him of his pistol, which he pressed against the man's head.

During that brief distraction, Shade had pulled his spare pistol from his boot and was now standing beside the general, his arm around the man's throat, the pistol pressed against his temple.

"If everyone remains calm," he said in a quiet voice more deadly than the loudest shout, "no one will get hurt."

"Rachel?"

"Yes, Shade?"

"Take the guns and the keys from those other two goons and lock them in that cell."

With fingers that shook only slightly, Rachel pulled the pistols from the black leather holsters. She was unable to hide her distaste at being forced to touch such deadly weapons, but reminded herself that these men had been prepared to kill. She did as instructed, breathing a sigh of relief as Conlan pushed himself up from the floor, relieved her of the ugly guns and gestured for his prisoner to follow. Seconds later the three were safely locked behind bars.

Which left General Rutskoya.

"Go ahead," Shade suggested, reading the general's mind. "Try and make a break for it. I'd love the excuse to put a bullet right through your head."

"You'll never get out of the country alive," the general warned. "Not with these two slowing you down." He shot a scornful expression Conlan and Rachel's way. "A cripple." He spat at Con's feet. "And a woman."

"My brother," Shade corrected. "And my wife-to-be."

Damn, this wasn't how he'd intended to propose. Shade had planned the scenario in careful detail. Once they were safely in Montacroix, he was going to take her out for a romantic candlelight dinner. Then a night on the town at the royal casino, then dancing. Afterward, they'd return to her room, where he'd have arranged with Burke to have a bottle of champagne from the royal vineyards waiting on ice.

They'd drink a toast to the successful outcome of their mission. To life. And love. Then, while violinists serenaded them from the courtyard below the balcony, he would ask her to marry him. Rachel would undoubtedly cry a little, but she'd accept, and then they'd make love. All night long.

It would be, Shade considered, the perfect ending to a perfect evening. And a perfect beginning of their life together. So what the hell had he done? Blurted it out under the very worst of situations, like a lovesick schoolboy.

And if that wasn't bad enough, the stricken expression on Rachel's face was definitely not encouraging. Why the hell was she looking at him that way? She should be happy. Hell, didn't most women dream of marriage?

"Your whore, you mean," the general said evilly. "Women are easy to come by, Shade. Why don't you leave the bitch with me?"

"Shut your goddamn mouth," Shade growled. "Before I do it for you."

"Perhaps we ought to ask the lovely Ms. Parrish if she'd like to stay. She doesn't look all that eager to enter into matrimonial bliss with you, Shade," the general observed.

Damn Rutskoya to hell. He was right. What was wrong with her?

While Shade was distracted, the general proved that he hadn't gotten where he was by being stupid. There was a flash of steel as the stiletto he kept up his sleeve slashed at Shade. Only razor-sharp instincts kept Shade from getting his throat cut.

"Dammit!" Pent-up fury, along with a building fear that he'd misjudged Rachel, burst free. He swung, hitting Rutskoya with the pistol across the face. The ugly sound of bone shattering mingled with the general's scream of pain. He dropped the stiletto to cover his broken nose. Blood gushed from between his fingers as if from a geyser.

And then they were on the ground and Shade was sitting on top of Rutskoya, pounding his fists into the already battered face. Right. Left. Right. Left. Over and over again.

All the pain this brutal man had caused him flashed through Shade's mind. All the pain he'd caused Conlan, not to mention Marianne's distress at a time when she should be experiencing the joy of being pregnant.

All the innocent people the general has tortured and killed seemed to be crying out in Shade's head for revenge.

But one voice rang out the loudest. The clearest.

"Please, Shade," Rachel begged. "If you truly love me, don't kill him. Please. Leave the judging to others!"

Dammit, Shade realized he could deny this woman nothing. Amazingly, love for Rachel had so taken over his heart that there was no longer any room for hate.

He ceased his brutal blows and looked up at her. Tears were streaming down her lovely face. He saw both love and terror in her soft gray eyes.

"The only reason I'm not killing him here and now, the way he deserves, is because of you," Shade said. "I want that understood."

Wiping at the free-falling tears with the backs of her hands, Rachel nodded. The lump in her throat prevented her from speaking.

Believing she'd finally prevailed just in time, Rachel gasped as he lifted the pistol. But rather than shoot the supine general, Shade merely knocked the man unconscious.

"He deserves to die, dammit," Shade muttered as he dragged the general into an adjoining cell and locked it.

"That's not for you to judge, Shade," Conlan said quietly, unknowingly echoing what Rachel had been telling him for days.

Rachel turned to Shade. "Thank you." Her relief was so palpable, Shade felt as if he could reach over and touch it.

As they made their way out of the prison, Rachel was surprised to find that she was still on earth. She'd expected to be called home the moment her mission was accomplished.

They managed to escape the compound, driving to the railroad station. They could not risk returning to the inn, Shade explained. Not when there was a chance the general could be discovered before morning. Nor could they risk trying to drive out of the country in the recognizable Mercedes. The partisans would repaint the car and return it to Montacroix later.

When they arrived at the station, Franja, Zdeslav and Duha's buxom, gorgeous daughter, was waiting with a new set of papers and a change of clothing for Rachel and both men. Although the baggy cotton slacks and oversized peasant blouse were not as fashionable as the mistress clothes Liz had selected for her, Rachel was grateful to be able to rid herself of the uniform that stood as a symbol of such cruel military repression.

After ten tension-filled minutes waiting on the platform, the train arrived. They boarded without incident and as they crossed the countryside, heading back into the Alps toward the Yaznovian-Montacroix border, Rachel realized she was exhausted. Unaccustomed to such bursts of adrenaline, she was now drained.

"It's going to take us a few hours to get to the border," Shade told her. "Why don't you take a nap?"

"I'm fine." Knowing that their precious time together was slipping away, Rachel did not want to waste a single moment sleeping.

Her ragged smile did not fool him. "You're a helluva lot better than fine, angel." Putting his arm around her, he coaxed her head onto his shoulder.

As his broad hand stroked her hair, Rachel breathed a soft, shimmering sigh of pleasure. Her eyelids fluttered shut. Within moments, she was asleep.

On the other side of the small private compartment, Conlan dozed, as well, leaving Shade to contemplate how much his life had changed in such a short time. The woman asleep in his arms was not only beautiful, she was intelligent and brave and as cool under pressure as any professional he'd ever met.

She was perfect. And, he thought with a burst of purely masculine possessiveness, she was his. All his.

They were going to get away with it. The soft glimmer of dawn was hovering on the horizon, tinting the Alpine glaciers a glistening pink and gold as the train approached the border station. The squeal of the brakes brought Rachel out of her deep sleep.

"I'm still here," she murmured in surprise as she found herself looking up into Shade's emerald eyes. Sometime during the journey, he'd arranged her so she was lying with her head in his lap.

"You didn't think I'd let you get away, did you?"

He was looking down at her with such love, Rachel almost burst into tears. How could she ever say goodbye?

Although she'd only wanted to help Shade, she fretted that she was going to end up hurting him after all. For all his life he'd operated on a single ideology of distrust. And although such cynicism had always saddened her, it had, in its own way, protected Shade's heart from pain.

But she had changed all that. She'd gotten him to open up, to let another person in. She'd taught him to not only trust but to love.

And what was his reward for such a dramatic character change? He was going to be abandoned. Again.

"We made it." He brushed a few strands of honey hair away from her cheeks with a cloud-soft touch.

Rachel managed a smile. "Thanks to you."

"And you." He dipped his head and kissed her. "We make one helluva team, Sister Rachel."

She longed to tell him the truth, to assure him that whatever happened, she would always, for eternity, love him. Despite the fact that Conlan was in the compartment with them, pretending intense interest in the scenery outside the window, she almost risked it.

But then the train had come to a screeching halt and the conductor was outside the door of their compartment, instructing all passengers to disembark.

"It's standard procedure," Shade assured Rachel. "The general isn't wild about his citizens leaving Yaznovia, so passengers have to pass through a border check before they can enter Montacroix." He kissed her again, briefly, but with a flare of emotion so strong it scorched her to the core. "It'll be all right," he promised. "*We'll* be all right."

They joined the procession of sleepy passengers making their way in a ragged line toward the two armed guards at the border. Across the wire fence, Rachel saw Prince Burke and his brother-in-law, Caine O'Bannion, standing beside a silver Bentley. An ambulance bearing the international symbol of the Rescue the Children Fund was parked nearby.

"Zdeslav and Duha contacted them after the train left the station," Shade answered Rachel's questioning look. He put his arm around her shoulders and squeezed. "Two more minutes, sweetheart. And we're home free."

He'd no sooner spoken when one of the guards turned in their direction. From his expression, it was apparent that he recognized Shade.

Later Caine would tell Shade that from that frozen instant of recognition, everything appeared to happen in slow motion.

The guard raised his rifle, pointing it at Shade. He pulled the trigger. A shot rang out.

That's when Rachel, responding the only way she knew how, threw herself in front of the man she loved. Blood darkened the back of her blouse. "Rachel!" As she slumped in his arms, Shade cried out.

Before the guard could get off another shot, a group of armed freedom fighters came surging out of the woods, effectively holding the border guards at bay while Shade carried Rachel across the border into Montacroix.

The instant he reached the other side, he dropped to his knees, cradling her against him, praying to a God he'd never believed in to save her.

He thought his prayers were answered when she opened her eyes and with obvious effort, lifted a palm to his tortured face.

"I love you," she whispered through lips that had gone as dry as dust.

"And I love you." He covered her face with kisses, he rocked her in his arms. "You're going to be all right, Rachel." He brushed her hair away from her ashen face, he stroked her rapidly cooling flesh.

"And we're going to be married and have lots of kids and I'll teach them to fish in the creek behind the house, and we'll all take long walks in the woods. We'll even get a dog. What would you say about a golden retriever? They're supposed to be good with kids. . . .

"Shade." Conlan put his hand on Shade's shoulder. "It's too late."

"No!" Unaware of the tears streaming down his face, Shade pulled her more tightly against his chest, as if protecting her from harm. "It's not too late, dammit! She's going to be all right, Con. She has to be."

"I'm sorry." Conlan's own gentle eyes were wet. "But she's gone, Shade. Rachel's dead."

Immersed in their own grief, neither Shade nor Conlan noticed Joshua, dressed in the navy blue uniform of a Yaznovian train conductor, watching soberly from the sidelines.

13

RACHEL WAS BURIED in Vermont.

In a centuries-old cemetery not far from his house. Shade visited every day, bringing bouquets of lilacs and daffodils and tulips.

The flowers were a harbinger of spring. They promised days of sunshine and warmth. But inside his heart, except for that small pocket where Rachel continued to dwell, Shade could feel only cold.

In an attempt to work off his lingering depression, anger and sorrow, he spent his days clearing his overgrown land, wielding saw and ax and shovel until he could barely lift his arms. Then he fell into bed, into a sleep tortured with dreams—vivid, wonderful, horrible dreams of his too-brief time with Rachel.

The only bright spot in his life was the news report out of Yaznovia of an earthquake near the village stronghold of the general. Although the civilians miraculously escaped injury, the general's car, the report continued, was buried beneath tons of rock that had fallen from the Alpine cliffs.

Remembering what Rachel had said about letting others do the judging, Shade knew the general finally had gotten his well-deserved comeuppance.

There were also reports that the partisan leader had taken over the palace and declared that free elections would soon be held.

"I suppose that's good news," Shade said. He was sitting beside Rachel's grave.

Although he knew some people might think him crazy, Shade talked to Rachel often—when he first got up in the morning, during the day while he worked, at night when he lay in his too-lonely bed.

Unable to forget the story she'd told him, Shade traveled to Salem, to the Charter Street cemetery. The burial ground was a dark and moody place with weather-beaten granite headstones dating back to the seventeenth century. On the other side of the iron fence, tucked into a small site beside the cemetery, surrounded by a rustic stone wall that was erected as part of the city's tercentenary commemoration in 1992, was what he'd come to see.

A small park had been created as a memorial to the twenty people executed for witchcraft in that crazy, bloody summer of 1692.

The park was both serene and disquieting at the same time. Inscriptions had been carved into the stone threshold, futile protestations of innocence made during the trials, poignant prayers, desperate pleas that disappeared beneath the wall, just as the truth had been crushed that long-ago summer. The trees planted amid the spring-green grass were black locusts, the kind, Shade read from his guidebook, from which some of the victims had been hung. The ground dipped down at the far end of the grassy space so that the grave markers in the cemetery appeared to be peering in through the iron bars of the fence, as steadfastly silent as those citizens of old Salem who had stood by and allowed their neighbors to die.

Along the wall were twenty cantilevered stone slabs, meant to act as benches. Into each slab had been carved the name of one of the witch-hunt's victims.

His heart pounding in his throat, Shade walked slowly around the perimeter of the park, reading each name and the date of the victim's death. On the other side of the small grassy area, a teacher was telling a class of eight-year-olds all the reasons it was important to remember what had happened on Gallows Hill.

Years ago, Shade had visited the Vietnam memorial in Washington and had been struck by the mute power of all those names. This small memorial was proving no less potent.

Then he saw it. *Rachel Parrish. Midwife. Hanged. July 25, 1692.*

"Oh, my God." Shade groaned and closed his eyes.

"Excuse me." A soft voice beside him asked, "Are you all right?"

Startled, he glanced down, half-expecting to find Rachel smiling up at him. But instead it was the young teacher, concern visible in her eyes.

"I'm fine. This is all just a little rough to take."

"It is a bit overwhelming, the first time," she agreed.

"You come here often?" How could she stand it? Shade wondered. He could almost hear the victims' cries. Rachel's cries.

"I'm a historian of the trials." She gestured toward a neighboring bench. "Susan Martin was an ancestor of mine. She was murdered for trying to overturn her father's will," she revealed in a dry tone.

"What do you know about Rachel Parrish?"

"Ah, Rachel." The woman ran her fingers over the carved name just as Shade had done. "Poor Rachel committed the terrible crime of being ahead of her time. She had the audacity to believe that childbirth was something natural, and not a punishment from God brought down on women because of Eve biting into that forbidden apple. That was, of course, a heretical idea to the Puritan establishment.

"When she attempted to ease the pain of labor, she was declared in league with the devil. She could have confessed and been freed, of course—"

"But she was too damn stubborn to recant," Shade interrupted brusquely.

The teacher glanced up at him, clearly curious at the mix of frustration and anger in his tone. "Rachel was innocent," she said quietly. "There were a great many people arrested that summer. The only victims killed were those who refused to 'confess.' I admire them for that, even though I'm not certain I'd have the nerve to stand up to torture myself."

"Rachel Parrish was a remarkable woman."

She smiled. "Was she a relative?"

"Close," Shade answered. God, they'd come so very close.

A commotion beneath one of the trees, as two boys, tossing a Red Sox baseball cap belonging to a third back and forth in a game of keep-away, halted the conversation. The teacher returned to her class, leaving Shade to stand beside Rachel's bench for a long, thoughtful time.

Although the idea flew in the face of everything logical, everything he'd been taught during those long, dry sermons in the chapel of the Vermont boys' home, Shade knew that the woman he'd loved then lost, and the brave, stubborn woman who refused to swear a false oath even to save her own life, were the same person.

He'd known she was special.

He just hadn't realized how special.

A soft spring breeze began blowing off the harbor, ruffling the leaves. Shade felt something brush against his cheek. Something that could have been the wind.

But he knew that it was his angel. Comforting him as she'd done that icy Vermont Christmas Day.

He shut his eyes hard and realized that until now, he'd never known that it was possible to feel both joy and sorrow at the same time.

THE FOLLOWING SUNDAY dawned bright and gloriously sunny.

Shade was out in the yard, planting a tree beside his deck. An oak, in memory of Rachel, the only woman he'd ever loved. The only woman he would ever love. The woman, as irrationally as it might sound to others, he knew he would someday be with again.

He was tapping the earth around the roots, when he looked up and saw her. Running toward him, wearing a somber dark dress so like the one she'd been wearing when they'd first met.

"Rachel?"

At first he believed she was a dream. Born of his aching need.

"Oh, Shade!"

As Rachel flung herself into his arms, he realized, with a burst of pure joy, that she was unbelievably, wonderfully real.

"How? Why? What are you doing here?" he asked between kisses.

"There's so much to tell, I don't know where to begin."

"I want to hear everything. Later."

Crying and laughing at the same time, Rachel clung to him as he carried her into the house. "Later," she agreed breathlessly.

Afraid she would be taken away from him again at any instant, he took her directly to the bedroom and laid her atop the patchwork quilt with reverent care. The room was washed with warm, buttery spring sunshine.

Rachel drew him down beside her and wrapped her arms around him, seeking the solid feel of him, the warmth, the rightness of his body against hers. She laughed breathlessly, then kissed him deeply, revealing a boldness, a confidence that allowed her to come to him freely with her own needs and demands.

Because it seemed an eternity since they'd been together, because their mutual, desperate need was so strong, they undressed each other hurriedly. Shade whisked away Rachel's dress, tearing first it, and then her underwear, before she could catch her breath. Just as quickly, she stripped him of his jeans and shirt and cotton briefs.

Her lips raced over his throat. Her breasts pressed against his chest. Her need was incendiary. His was equally hot and every bit as urgent. In one strong move, Shade lifted her as if she were weightless, which indeed at this moment she felt she was, then brought her swiftly back down, plunging into her.

Rachel cried out in rapturous pleasure. His long fingers dug into her waist, holding her tightly. Her knees pressed against his body as she moved with him, harder and faster, pushing each other to a place they'd never gone before. A place beyond the normal realms of time and space, where love and desire ruled.

Through the thunder in his head, Shade heard Rachel call his name. They'd reached the pinnacle and were hovering on the razor's edge between reason and madness.

Holding her tightly, gasping her name, Shade closed his mouth over hers, let himself go and welcomed the madness.

Afterward, he lay with her atop the rumpled quilt and prayed that if this was just another of the erotic dreams he'd been having lately, he'd never, ever wake up.

"That was," she murmured, "beautiful." She pressed her lips against his damp chest. "Almost as beautiful as that tree you just planted."

"Beautiful," he agreed. Tearing his eyes away from her lush, warm body, he followed her gaze out the window, toward the leaves of the newly planted tree—bright green leaves signifying promise. He ran his hand down her hair, playing with the thick blond strands that were still moist from their frantic lovemaking.

"Tell me you're not a dream. Or a mirage."

"I'm most definitely real." She wiggled teasingly against him and slanted him a dangerously seductive smile. "Can't you tell?"

"It's hard to believe. When I brought you in here, for a moment, I was almost afraid to touch you. I was afraid my hand would go right through you."

She lifted his hand to her lips and kissed each fingertip. "But it didn't."

"No."

"Surely my coming back can't be harder to believe than everything else you've had to accept lately?"

That was, Shade decided, the understatement of the millennium. "I went to Salem."

"I know." She'd hoped he would and had cried when he had.

"It's true, isn't it?" He lifted a few more strands of hair, arranging them over her bare shoulders, her breasts. "Everything you tried to tell me. About Salem. The trials. Joshua. All of it."

"Yes."

"God." He shook his head. "I thought I'd lost you forever."

The pain in his voice tore at Rachel's tender heart. She sat up and wrapped her arms around her bent legs. "That was a terrible mistake." She looked into his eyes. Dark green eyes that revealed the deep wounds her death had inflicted. "I was only supposed to be wounded."

"But you died, dammit. I was holding you in my arms. I felt your breath slip away."

"I know. And I'm so horribly sorry you were hurt, but you see, although it was totally against policy, Joshua responded with pure emotion, rather than logic, and plucked my spirit out of my body to prevent me from suffering."

"Dammit, if it was all a mistake, if you were supposed to stay here with me, where the hell have you been all these weeks?"

His gritty tone didn't disturb her. Rachel much preferred Shade's irritation to his earlier pain. "I wanted to return sooner, but Joshua and I were brought before a judicial review board for having broken so many celestial rules."

"You had to go through another trial?" he asked unbelievingly. "After everything you went through the first time?"

"It wasn't at all the same," she hastened to assure him. "In fact, as soon as the board decreed that Joshua wouldn't lose his angelic ranking, I was given permission to return to you."

His fingers slid into her hair as he framed her face, holding her gaze to his. "For how long?" he asked cautiously, trying to tell himself that he'd be grateful for any brief time they'd been given, but wanting an eternity.

Reading the concern etched onto his ruggedly handsome face, Rachel's heart went out to him. "I was thinking," she said, her silver eyes laughing, "of seventy or eighty years. If you think you can put up with a stubborn, headstrong wife for that long."

Shade began laughing, as well. He'd never felt so good. So free. "I'll give it my best shot."

She pressed her hand against her chest. "Such a romantic proposal." She sighed dramatically. "It makes my heart go all pitter-pat."

"Give me a few more minutes to get my strength up again and I'll see to it your entire body goes pitter-pat," Shade promised.

Rachel knew from experience that he could and it would. She glanced down at her clothing, scattered across the floor, knowing that her dress was ripped beyond repair. Not that she cared. If the truth be told, she hated the ugly dark dress Joshua had sent her back to earth in.

"I don't have anything to wear," she murmured.

"We'll go shopping," Shade promised. "In a few days."

She arched a brow. "That long?"

"We have a lot of catching up to do," he reminded her. "And it's ten miles to the nearest town."

She smiled. "You just want to keep me naked."

"That, too," he said agreeably.

Rachel laughed, as she was supposed to. "You know," she said, suddenly serious, "I probably should have warned you that I'll only agree to marry you on the condition that you promise to stay out of trouble. No more running off to all the world's hot spots and leaving your wife and children at home."

Children. After Rachel's death, Shade had thought he was destined to go through life without ever knowing what it would be like to be a father. Because there'd only been one woman he'd ever wanted to have children with.

"You've got yourself a deal. As it happens, Caine O'Bannion is opening up a New England branch of his security company. And you're looking at the new regional vice president."

"I hadn't known." Incredibly, the deal must have come through while she'd been arguing Joshua's case before the judicial board.

"It isn't dangerous work," Shade assured her. "It's strictly white-collar, business-oriented stuff. I won't have to travel, the hours are routine, and the vacation benefits are more than generous.

"Which will give me," Shade promised as he kissed Rachel, "plenty of time to spend with my angelic wife and all the children we're going to have together."

"Oh, I do like the idea of a large family," Rachel agreed happily as the kisses grew longer. And deeper.

"Speaking of progeny—" his lips plucked at hers as his hands moved between them "—what would you say to spending the rest of the day making a baby?"

His clever, wicked touch was making her melt all over again. To think she'd been granted a lifetime of such glorious lovemaking! Twining her arms around his neck, Rachel surrendered to the pleasure. To Shade.

"I'd say yes," she agreed breathlessly.

As he pulled her down beside him and began to make love to her again, a thought occurred to Rachel. A wonderful, brilliant, thrilling idea.

"Shade, darling?"

"Mmm?" He ran his thumb over the rosy tip of her breast and felt her breath quicken.

"May I ask you a question?"

She was so soft. So sweet. He lifted his head, looked straight into her laughing, loving eyes and knew that he'd just discovered paradise on earth.

"One question. But you'd better make it quick." Although he'd vowed to make things last this time, explosions were already bombarding his system, from his brain to his loins.

"Quick," Rachel agreed on a gasp as his teeth captured a sensitive nipple and she felt herself rapidly slipping back into that smoky world she'd only ever known with Shade.

"How does one go about getting a midwife's license in Vermont?"

INDULGE A LITTLE 6947 SWEEPSTAKES
NO PURCHASE NECESSARY

HERE'S HOW THE SWEEPSTAKES WORKS:
The Harlequin Reader Service shipments for January, February and March 1994 will contain, respectively, coupons for entry into three prize drawings: a trip for two to San Francisco, an Alaskan cruise for two and a trip for two to Hawaii. To be eligible for any drawing using an Entry Coupon, simply complete and mail according to directions.

There is no obligation to continue as a Reader Service subscriber to enter and be eligible for any prize drawing. You may also enter any drawing by hand printing your name and address on a 3" x 5" card and the destination of the prize you wish that entry to be considered for (i.e., San Francisco trip, Alaskan cruise or Hawaiian trip). Send your 3" x 5" entries to: Indulge a Little 6947 Sweepstakes, c/o Prize Destination you wish that entry to be considered for, P.O. Box 1315, Buffalo, NY 14269-1315, U.S.A. or Indulge a Little 6947 Sweepstakes, P.O. Box 610, Fort Erie, Ontario L2A 5X3, Canada.

To be eligible for the San Francisco trip, entries must be received by 4/30/94; for the Alaskan cruise, 5/31/94; and the Hawaiian trip, 6/30/94. No responsibility is assumed for lost, late or misdirected mail. Sweepstakes open to residents of the U.S. (except Puerto Rico) and Canada, 18 years of age or older. All applicable laws and regulations apply. Sweepstakes void wherever prohibited.

For a copy of the Official Rules, send a self-addressed, stamped envelope (WA residents need not affix return postage) to: Indulge a Little 6947 Rules, P.O. Box 4631, Blair, NE 68009, U.S.A.

INDR93

INDULGE A LITTLE 6947 SWEEPSTAKES
NO PURCHASE NECESSARY

HERE'S HOW THE SWEEPSTAKES WORKS:
The Harlequin Reader Service shipments for January, February and March 1994 will contain, respectively, coupons for entry into three prize drawings: a trip for two to San Francisco, an Alaskan cruise for two and a trip for two to Hawaii. To be eligible for any drawing using an Entry Coupon, simply complete and mail according to directions.

There is no obligation to continue as a Reader Service subscriber to enter and be eligible for any prize drawing. You may also enter any drawing by hand printing your name and address on a 3" x 5" card and the destination of the prize you wish that entry to be considered for (i.e., San Francisco trip, Alaskan cruise or Hawaiian trip). Send your 3" x 5" entries to: Indulge a Little 6947 Sweepstakes, c/o Prize Destination you wish that entry to be considered for, P.O. Box 1315, Buffalo, NY 14269-1315, U.S.A. or Indulge a Little 6947 Sweepstakes, P.O. Box 610, Fort Erie, Ontario L2A 5X3, Canada.

To be eligible for the San Francisco trip, entries must be received by 4/30/94; for the Alaskan cruise, 5/31/94; and the Hawaiian trip, 6/30/94. No responsibility is assumed for lost, late or misdirected mail. Sweepstakes open to residents of the U.S. (except Puerto Rico) and Canada, 18 years of age or older. All applicable laws and regulations apply. Sweepstakes void wherever prohibited.

For a copy of the Official Rules, send a self-addressed, stamped envelope (WA residents need not affix return postage) to: Indulge a Little 6947 Rules, P.O. Box 4631, Blair, NE 68009, U.S.A.

INDR93

INDULGE A LITTLE

SWEEPSTAKES

OFFICIAL ENTRY COUPON

This entry must be received by: APRIL 30, 1994
This month's winner will be notified by: MAY 15, 1994
Trip must be taken between: JUNE 30, 1994-JUNE 30, 1995

YES, I want to win the San Francisco vacation for two. I understand that the prize includes round-trip airfare, first-class hotel, rental car and pocket money as revealed on the "wallet" scratch-off card.

Name______________________________________

Address _________________________ Apt. ____________

City_______________________________________

State/Prov.____________________ Zip/Postal Code____________

Daytime phone number_____________________________
(Area Code)

Account #______________________________________

Return entries with invoice in envelope provided. Each book in this shipment has two entry coupons—and the more coupons you enter, the better your chances of winning!

 MONTH1

INDULGE A LITTLE

SWEEPSTAKES

OFFICIAL ENTRY COUPON

This entry must be received by: APRIL 30, 1994
This month's winner will be notified by: MAY 15, 1994
Trip must be taken between: JUNE 30, 1994-JUNE 30, 1995

YES, I want to win the San Francisco vacation for two. I understand that the prize includes round-trip airfare, first-class hotel, rental car and pocket money as revealed on the "wallet" scratch-off card.

Name______________________________________

Address _________________________ Apt. ____________

City_______________________________________

State/Prov.____________________ Zip/Postal Code____________

Daytime phone number_____________________________
(Area Code)

Account #______________________________________

Return entries with invoice in envelope provided. Each book in this shipment has two entry coupons—and the more coupons you enter, the better your chances of winning!

© 1993 HARLEQUIN ENTERPRISES LTD. MONTH1